CUT GUAVAS

ALSO BY ROBERT ANTONI

Divina Trace (1991)

Blessed is the Fruit (1997)

My Grandmother's Erotic Tales (2000)

Carnival (2005)

As Flies to Whatless Boys (2013)

ROBERT ANTONI

"CUT GUAVAS"

OR . . .

"POSTSCRIPT TO THE CIVILIZATION OF THE SIMIANS"

A NOVEL

SHAPESHIFTING AS A SCREENPLAY

PEEPAL TREE

First published in Great Britain in 2018
Peepal Tree Press Ltd
17 King's Avenue
Leeds LS6 1QS
England

ISBN 9781845234294

Supported using public funding by
ARTS COUNCIL
ENGLAND

for

Austin Stoker

Derek Walcott

&

Barack Obama

Our Three in One

So let's kick off the era of unfilmable scenarios . . .

Benjamin Fondane, preface,
THREE SCENARIOS, CINEPOEMS
(including a surrealist photograph
of the author "mutating" by Man Ray)

"And here's a note in pencil. 'Rejection slip sent 11-26-47. No self-addressed envelope.
For the Incinerator' - twice underlined."

Aldous Huxley
APE AND ESSENCE

If my father hadn't exactly disappointed me, he remained something unknown,
something volatile and vaguely threatening.

Barack Hussein Obama II
DREAMS FROM MY FATHER

Fanfiction is defined by being both related to its subject's canonical fictional universe (referred to as "canon", and created by professional writers) while simultaneously existing outside of it.

Wikipedia, 23 March 2016

OPENING SEQUENCE

1

We hear, under the vibrating wire of ciçadas-shrill, early morning birds chirping.
We see, as the camera lens clicks into focus, the exterior shot of a modest, Spanish-
style home. As viewed from the street in a haze of bright sunshine - white stucco
walls and red, barrel-tiled roof. The front door is heavy plank wood, rounded
at the top, with a faux wrought-iron grille over the peephole. It opens into a
circular foyer - cocktail-umbrella roof above - offering the impression, from
the outside, of a swallowed-up tower. The yard shows unkempt grass, a few weeds,
ancient oak with mossy trunk and a small tire hanging by a length of old rope.
Parked in the driveway, a faded black Toyota, part of the rear bumper drooping.
Peeling and discolored "Obama, we'll never forget" bumper sticker. The house
in need of repair, mold-stained, with plaster coming away at the corners, roof
showing wear.

Superimpose card over grass in lower center of frame:

STUDIO CITY,
CALIFORNIA
2016 A.D.

Card dissolves, as the camera draws in slightly on the house.

2

Cut to an interior view of the small kitchen/dining room. The shot opens with a loud whistle of steam from the kettle on the stove. Its shrill diminishes, though, as AUSTIN STOKER, his back turned to us, pours hot water from the kettle into a chipped white enamel mug. He turns and takes a seat at the wrought-iron dining table behind him, with four matching iron chairs. Conspicuous on the table is a medium ziplock bag containing a fist-sized gnarl of dried herb; also a wicker basket with bananas, and a plastic prescription medicine vial. Austin wears black, unembellished track pants, a black tee-shirt, lightweight charcoal wind-breaker, plain running shoes.

He pulls open the ziplock and slowly adds pinches of the herb to the steaming water in the mug. After a while he takes up the ziplock, forms a funnel with it, and dumps in the entire mound. Some spilling out onto the table, which Austin carefully pinches up and adds to the mug, with a few brown branches of the herb sticking out at the top.

He raises his mug, blows into it, and cautiously takes a sip - grimacing.

Meanwhile his wife, ROBIN - still in her nightrobe, pajamas and bedroom slippers - has entered the kitchen behind him. She fixes herself coffee from the coffeemaker on the counter in the background, her back turned.

As Austin takes another prolonged, boisterous sip and frowns, we hear her voice - still groggy with sleep.

"What died?"

She turns and takes a seat at the table facing him.

Robin is African-American, slight Southern accent, early 60s, with a vivacious personality. She's an entertainment industry lawyer.

Austin is 83, young-looking for his age, a sienna-skinned black man – athletic, fluid in his movements. There's something recognizably foreign in his features – Cuban? Puerto Rican? – it's difficult to place. Austin was among the first black actors to infiltrate Hollywood during the 60s and 70s, achieving moderate success. For his early roles he is recognized by film enthusiasts as something of an icon.

  *

Due to the limited number of parts available for blacks in major motion pictures, together with the film industry's history of entrenched racism, Austin's roles have been restricted to minor characters, generally stereotypes – with the latter achieving its fullest expression in the Blaxploitation films of the 70s.

---

* ASSAULT ON PRECINCT 13 is a 1976 American action thriller film written, directed, scored and edited by John Carpenter. It stars Austin Stoker as a police officer who defends a defunct precinct against an attack by a relentless criminal gang, along with Darwin Joston as a convicted murderer who helps him ... ASSAULT initially met with mixed reviews and unimpressive box-office returns in the United States. However when the film premiered in the 1977 London Film Festival it received an ecstatic review by festival director Ken Wlaschin. This led to critical acclaim first in Britain, and then throughout Europe. It gained a considerable cult following, reappraisal from critics, and was later reevaluated in America as one of the best action films of its era and of Carpenter's career. (Wikipedia, 27 April 2016)

ASSAULT trailer: www.robertantoni.com/assault

Austin has managed, nonetheless, to elevate these roles, lending them dignity and authority. In recent years it has become increasingly difficult for him to find work.

He takes another extended, noisy sip from his mug, then clenches his teeth. His face relaxes, as he looks over at Robin.

"I think it's my hippocampus that croaked," he says.

Robin draws her words out – like she's not ready to wake up yet. Not ready to decipher Austin's early a.m. cogitations.

"Your who?"

He continues undeterred.

"My brain-seahorse. Named by a 16th Century Venetian anatomist, Julius Maximos something-or-other ... it's the part responsible for both short and long-term memory."

Austin raises his mug to her.

"But this stuff'll fix me up."

She tenses her forehead, skeptical.

"Smells disgusting."

"Ashwagandha in Sanskrit. Means 'odor of a sweaty horse' – big horse cures a little horse, I guess."

He takes a sip, contorts his face again.

"Tastes worse than it smells."

Robin rolls her eyes at him.

"This something else you heard about on the internet? You got too much time on your hands, Austin."

"Mummy called this her memory tea – her bush medicine. She knew the plant by its African name, koorshout. Mummy drank this tea every morning till the day she passed, like her mother before her."

He sips, grimaces.

"As I told the doctor – dementia's just something we got in our genes."

She takes a deep breath, looks at him soberly.

"Nothing's written in stone, Austin. Nucleotides either."

Robin says it like she's punching back softly at him, adding, " . . . if I remember my high school biology chapter on DNA right."

"Yeah," he backpedals. "But – "

She cuts him off.

"Besides, science's come a long way since your momma's time."

Austin pauses a few beats, considers this.

"Well, it better had," he says. "Cause one thing for sure – an actor's not worth much without his memory . . . IF he can find employment, that is."

She tries to shift the subject.

"So where'd you get the bush from? Some ganja dealer?"

"The Trini herb-vender at Farmers Market. Took me forever to find it, and it cost me a fortune – $75 a gram! The really good stuff has to've grown on a termites' nest – Mummy always swore to that."

Robin looks at him with her eyebrows compressed, mouth an O.

"Hold on a sec ... you really believe that bush – whatever it is – grew on a termites' nest?"

"Sure. Vendor knew exactly what I was talking about – her Hindu 'amma' used to drink it too."

Robin shakes her head, resigned.

"Then you're not only gullible, you're living in the dark ages."

"The age of wisdom and magic!" he says with verve.

"Superstition and witchcraft," she counters with equal strike-back. "All due respect to your momma."

Robin sips from her mug, gestures with it.

"How bout some coffee? Hand ground with a stone by some ancient and exploited Guatemalan woman?"

She smiles, "Sarcasm intended."

"I'll get it at the coffee shop ... I'm meeting up with a couple of the boys to run though our lines."

"Yeah?" she's cautiously curious.

"Got a call from Harry yesterday. They're finally doing that ASSAULT sequel, after forty-three years."

"Really?"

Austin grins – proud of himself, much as he tries to hide it.

"D'you believe?"

"Hold on ... " Robin is momentarily confused. "Which ASSAULT film?"

Austin clarifies.

"The SIMIAN one. Harry wants pretty much the same cast – those of us that're still kickin'."

"That's amazing, Austin." She pauses, absorbing this. "Been forever since you got a half-decent part."

After a breath she adds, "In a bona fide movie, that is."

He smiles too.

"Rather have my teeth bashed in . . . than do another Poligrip commercial."

Austin contorts his face, mimicking himself.

" . . . now I can even eat spareribs n' cornpone without shame!"

"For real," she says with a half-frown.

Robin takes up the child-proof medicine vial, compresses and twists off the top. She places two blue pills on the table before him.

"Better take your meds then, baby. Cause somehow I trust the doctor a little more than your Trinidadian herb-vender."

"I'll stick to mummy's memory tea, thank you."

"Anyways, between the two of 'em," her tone is serious, "hopefully you'll remember your lines."

Austin looks down at the table - and they're both aware of the slight tremor in his lower lip. It's as though the oxygen has been sucked from the room.

"Hopefully I remember which century I'm living in," he says.

There's a tense silence. Robin suddenly feels she needs to rein the conversation in. She turns to him again.

"Hasn't gotten that bad. According to Doc, it's only Stage 2."

Another pause. Austin raises his face to her. He swallows hard, continues slowly.

"I'm embarrassed to tell you this, honey. But the fact is . . . I spent half-an-hour yesterday rummaging through our closet, looking for my imaginary overalls."

Robin shakes her head.

"You were looking for what?"

"Guess I thought I was Homer, that field-slave I played in ROOTS."

Her tone is a combination of not wanting to believe him, and not being able to.

"You're kidding," she says.

"Harry's phone call snapped me out of it."

She takes a breath.

"Better take your pills then, baby - cause I don't wanna come home and find you pickin' cotton in the front yard."

Austin smiles, relieved to have gotten it out.

"Maybe I'll be a gorilla swinging in the oak tree."

She sounds relieved, too.

"If Harry gives you a part."

Austin looks around the kitchen, like he's just thought of something.

"You see where I put that script?"

"You're sitting on it."

"Right." He gets up, exposing the script. "That's so I remember where I put it."

"I'll be late again today, baby."

Austin turns to her.

"Marvin Gaye suit?"

"We're representing Nona."

"'Blurred Lines' business?"

"Pharrell and Robin Thicke - couple of goons."* She rolls her eyes again. "Want me to pick up something for dinner on my way home?"

"Sure."

---

* "Blurred Lines" is a single written and performed by American recording artists Robin Thicke and Pharrell Williams. The song became the subject of a bitter legal dispute in March, 2016 with the Gaye family ... as to whether it infringed copyrights to "Got to Give It Up," by Marvin Gaye. (Wikipedia, 16 May 2016)

He bends to kiss her.

"Got your script?" she asks.

He takes it up. Also a banana from the basket.

"But it feels ... like I'm forgetting something else."

"You'll remember later."

"When I find my overalls!"

Robin reaches out and squeezes his shoulder. A brief but distinctly motherly gesture that feels odd, considering she's twenty years younger. She knows she's been doing it a lot lately.

Austin turns and steps out of the frame to our left.

As Robin raises her mug for another slow sip, she notices the two blue pills left on the table. She calls after him over her shoulder.

"Austin!"

She puts her mug down. And after a moment she turns her face to the camera, looking straight at us – but what Robin sees before her is a void, its uncertainty difficult to dismiss.

She shakes her head. Puts the pills back into the vial.

3

Exterior shot of Austin closing the heavy front door - with its rounded top
and rusted wrought-iron grille - behind him. He holds the banana in one hand,
slightly tattered script folded under his other arm.

The camera follows as he walks around to the side of the house, past the
Toyota with its sagging bumper, peeling and eating his banana. He tosses the skin
into a garbage can, then retrieves his bicycle that's leaning against the wall.
Austin drops the script in the front basket, climbs onto his bike in agile manner,
rides off.

We watch from behind as he peddles down the street. Just ahead a school
bus has stopped, its red lights slowly blinking, doors open, stop sign extended.
Before the neighboring house stands a white couple in their late thirties, with
their ten-year-old son. We see the boy quickly hug his parents and run off
toward the bus, wearing a Hulk backpack and carrying his Hulk lunchpail - the
boy dressed in shorts and white tee-shirt, high white socks and sneakers, his
navy L.A. Dodgers baseball cap turned backward on his head.

Close-up of Austin's face as he peddles past the school bus, red lights
blinking in a blur behind him.

Austin turns his head to look back over his shoulder, and the camera
shifts to his point-of-view.

Now we see that the neighbors standing before their home are transformed to
MAXIMOS and his wife EVA, the royal couple from ASSAULT ON THE CIVILIZATION OF
THE SIMIANS, in which Austin played the role of Anderson* - an African American
human who was Maximos' assistant, confidant and privileged advisor -

---

* although the part of Anderson is a leading role, Austin's name was not included
among the white (ape) stars in the film's opening credits

Maximos and Eva wear the same amateurish, dated prosthetic makeup of chimpanzees, and russet-colored tunics with loose trousers - exactly as Austin remembers them from the 1973 movie. The only addition is that Maximos and Eva now wear gaudy chains with medallions around their necks, featuring the body of the Hindu monkey-god, Hanuman, brandishing mace and mountain, with the face of Obama superimposed over the god's. Though from the distance we cannot make out the medallions' image precisely. We also see that the boy about to mount the bus steps is transformed to the girl-chimp MIRA, Maximos and Eva's daughter - Mira would have been the sister of Amadeus, their young son who was murdered by Gabo in the earlier film. She too wears the medallion (no cap).

In addition, we see through the bus windshield that the driver is "Scavenger Bob", who will appear later, wearing his red baseball cap and old-fashioned motorcycle goggles. He reaches his arm out of the driver's window, gently ringing a school hand-bell.

Maximos and Eva wave as Mira starts up the bus steps, wearing her Hulk backpack and carrying her Hulk lunchpail. But from Austin's and our point-of-view, it also appears that they are waving to HIM.

Cut to a reverse close-up of Austin: we see his face turn, seemingly unperturbed by the vision. As the camera pulls back to a long shot from behind and he continues pedaling down the street, the school bus in the lower left foreground with its red lights blinking, the driver ringing his hand-bell. The bus gradually edges out of the frame as the camera follows Austin riding his bicycle.

TITLES BEGIN (for Studio City story).

I

THE STORY

1

Open with a long shot from behind Austin on the right side of the frame, halting his bicycle before StarBucks.* On the left side of the road, over the long drive, we see a large, arching, wrought-iron gateway, "Metro-Goldwyn-Mayer" inscribed above the entrance. In the middle of the arch is the MGM logo, with a cat's head replacing the lion.

    In the distance we watch Austin park his bicycle in a stand in front of the StarBucks, and retrieve his script from the basket.

    Cut to an interior shot of Austin, approaching the coffeehouse counter. The attendant is a white boy with shaved head. He wears the franchise's forest-green bib apron and black tee-shirt, white sweatbands on his wrists like a basketball player. As the attendant leans forward onto his right hand beside the register, Austin notices what appears to be a purple swastika - peeking out from under the sweatband - tattooed onto the inside of his wrist.

    But when Austin blinks and looks again, the tattoo is gone. He shakes his head, speaks distractedly.

                    STOKER
          I'll take a grande cafe negro,
            two expresso shots.

               ATTENDANT
               (pauses)
          That two e's or one?

                  STOKER
           I said TWO.

               ATTENDANT
       (into microphone on counter)
            Grande neegro,
           two EX shots.

    Austin turns from the counter and takes a step - then turns around again, like he's forgotten something. He stares at the attendant belligerently.

---

* author uses Melville's original spelling of his character's name in his great American animal story, MOBY DICK

                    STOKER
                What the fuck
                was that?

                   ATTENDANT
            (smug look on his face)
                I'll bring it to
                your table, sir.

        Cut to a tracking shot of Austin, crossing the StarBucks to a table where
two of the actors from the simian ASSAULT are seated. They're older white men who,
forty-three years younger, starred in ape roles in the film: HOMER and VESUVIUS.*
Like Austin, they're dressed in their civvies. On the table before them are three
large paper cups of coffee, and three folded-open scripts similar to the one Austin
carries.

                    HOMER
                 (looks up)
              Hello, Austin.
            Slow start this morning?

                    STOKER
        (smiles, nods over at the coffee)
            My vehicle's in need of petrol.

                   VESUVIUS
               It's getting cold.

                    STOKER
          Let me tend to the prostate first
            - be with you boys in a second.

        We watch Austin approach the Men's Room, still carrying his script folded
under his arm. But before he can enter, Maximos (who he has just seen standing in
front of his home next door with his wife and daughter) exits, almost colliding
with Austin. He is still disguised as the chimpanzee.

                   MAXIMOS
                  Anderson!

----

*ASSAULT ON THE CIVILIZATION OF THE SIMIANS will be referred to as "ASSAULT"
throughout the script, and the proposed sequel, POSTSCRIPT TO THE CIVILIZATION OF
THE SIMIANS, will be referred to as "POSTSCRIPT". In addition, to avoid confusion,
Homer, Vesuvius - and all of the other actors except Austin - will be referred to
solely by their character names.

STOKER
Morning, Maximos.

Austin shuffles past him, unperturbed, and pushes into the Men's Room, "M" inscribed on the door.

2

The Men's Room door opens into a long shot of the CASTING STUDIO at MGM. In the
distance we see three older white men sitting in tall canvass folding-chairs.
Two hold scripts on their laps, and the other is smoking a cigar, ashing it into a
silver ashtray. One is the Director, the second the Casting Agent, and the third is
a Producer.

    The shot reverses to a close-up of Austin's face - he pauses for a moment,
shakes his head like he's clearing cobwebs away. He starts over toward the three
men, as the camera pulls back.

> CASTING AGENT
> (Austin approaches)
> Mr. Stoker.

> STOKER
> Morning, Harry.
> (nods to the other men)
> Mr. Thompson.
> Mr. Ross.

> CASTING AGENT
> I see you've got the script.

> STOKER
> Yes, sir.

> CASTING AGENT
> Let's try page 83. Could you
> give us your line at the bottom?

Austin flips to page 83, reads silently. He takes a breath, looks away for a
moment to summon his character, then looks directly at the casting agent.

> STOKER
> I guess you could say . . .
> they've finally ascended
> to the simian race.

There's a slight pause. The Director clears his throat.

                    DIRECTOR
              Let's try that again,
            this time give me Stoker.

                  CASTING AGENT
                   (confused)
              You mean Anderson.

                    DIRECTOR
              I mean what I say.
              I want STOKER.

Another pause. Austin repeats the line exactly as before.

                    STOKER
            I guess you could say ...
             they've finally ascended
              to the simian race.

                    DIRECTOR
                (enthusiastically)
            That's it, that's Stoker
              - we've got our man!

                  CASTING AGENT
             Thank you, Austin. Would you
            mind sticking around for an hour
             or so? We're ready to shoot.

                    STOKER
                Sure, Harry.
             Just one question -

                  CASTING AGENT
                     Yeah.

                    STOKER
          You guys got a gent's room in this place?
            My prostate's about to rupture!

                  CASTING AGENT
          (smiles, nods at the back of the room)
            Through the door back there.

As Austin turns toward the door he notices, presented on an easel half-hidden behind the three men, an artist's version of the publicity poster for the proposed sequel to the simian ASSAULT film.
    He turns around again to study it closer.

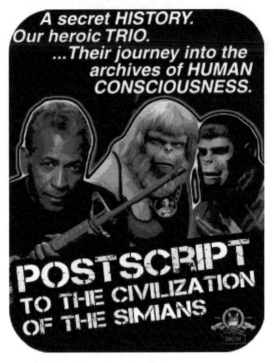

Austin stares at himself in the poster.
    After a moment he turns, untroubled, and walks toward the rest room, "WC" inscribed on the door.

                    CASTING AGENT
                      (offstage)
                  See you in an hour,
                       Anderson.

We watch him turn the knob and push the door in.

3

The rest-room door opens into a panoramic shot, from Austin's point-of-view, of Simian City. The shot begins on Austin's head and shoulders, as seen from behind, slowly edging him out. In the background, to the left side of the frame, we see forested mountains; to our right, vast desert. In the verdant valley nestled between them, we see the utopian arboreal city: orderly, elaborate, multilevel treehouses with terraces slung with hammocks, the houses accessed by vines and bamboo ladders. On the sloping plain between the arboreal city and the mountains in the distance are extensive, well-tended vegetable gardens and fruit orchards.

Superimpose card over dirt road in the lower center of frame:

NORTH AMERICA
2680 A.D.

Card fades as the camera pans, revealing Simian City to be the picture of organization, cooperation and primitive industry: ape farmers work the fields, female apes wash clothes and prepare food, a house is being built, the wheel of a wagon replaced, etc. - exactly as Austin remembers it from the 1973 movie. Though a decade has passed on the simian calendar since the termination of ASSAULT.* As in the earlier film, the majority of the inhabitants of the city are apes (chimpanzees, orangutans, gorillas). There's also a number of African American humans, young and old, collaborating with the apes, the human children and young chimps playing together - but now there's only the occasional Caucasian human. That's one notable difference between this Simian City and the city of ASSAULT: the considerably fewer number of white humans. Another significant difference is that now, though the city is still ruled by Maximos, the humans are no longer slaves, or even servants; they live and work peacefully as equals among the apes - Anderson's poignant entreaty to Maximos in the closing moments of ASSAULT. The other change is that all of the apes, in addition to the humans, young and old, now wear the bling medallions around their necks (the few white humans as well) emblazoned with the image of the Hanuman-Obama.

TITLES BEGIN (for Simian City story) followed by a pause.

The camera reverses to a long shot with Austin in the foreground, standing before a Johnny-on-the-Spot, still holding his script folded under his arm. In the distance behind him we make out the large white buildings of MGM Studios, indicating that this is a set. Closer, off to Austin's left, are several open-sided tents: under one a table is spread with food, another contains racks of ape costumes

---

* equivalent of forty-three human years

and a makeup artist at work, another with multiple television monitors and technicians. Beneath a larger tent is a long table surrounded by seated actors – talking, eating – some costumed as apes, others not. Between the tents and the Simian City set are multiple cameras, one craned, and sound recording equipment, all manned by technicians.

Close-up of Austin's face, composed, as he turns and starts over toward the tents.

Cut to a medium shot of the tent with the television monitors and technicians. To the right side of this tent are three tall canvass chairs, just as in the casting studio, where the Director is seated, the Casting Agent* and the Producer (still ashing his cigar into the silver ashtray).

                    DIRECTOR
              (as Austin approaches)
              We're shooting the
              "hereditary" scene.

                    STOKER
              (halts, remembers)
          Where Maximos convinces Anderson
            to go with him to Forbidden City
              in search of the tape?**

                  2nd DIRECTOR
                    Yeah.
                  You got it?

                    STOKER
                Sure, Harry –
            I'll report to costumes.

                    DIRECTOR
                  (tersely)
                You're perfect
                the way you are.

Austin looks down and considers his outfit, lightly grasping the lapels of his windbreaker in each hand. He looks up, confused.

                    STOKER
                    Really?

_____

* also the co-director, from this point referred to as 2nd Director
** actually the reverse of ASSAULT, where it's Anderson who convinces Maximos

                    DIRECTOR
             Just give me Stoker.

                  2nd DIRECTOR
             You mean Anderson.

                    DIRECTOR
                I mean what I
                fuckin' say.

                  2nd DIRECTOR
             (shakes his head)
                    O.K.

                    DIRECTOR
                Let's burn
             some celluloid!

4

Camera dissolves to an interior shot of Maximos' treehouse, slowly drawing in: Austin and Maximos (as chimpanzee) are seated on stools at a roughly-hewn dining table, surrounded by two other stools. Maximos is dressed as Austin remembers him from the previous ASSAULT film, in his russet-colored tunic and loose trousers. Austin still in his track pants and tee-shirt. On the table before them are two calabash cups and a clay jug, in addition to Austin's clipboard.* In the background, Eva (as chimpanzee) prepares food in the rudimentary but carefully organized kitchen, a faded forest-green bib apron tied around her waist over her tunic. She is helped by young Mira.

> MAXIMOS
> (takes a sip of wine)
> ... well there's only one
> way to find out.

> STOKER
> Meaning?

> MAXIMOS
> The tapes in the underground
> Archives of Forbidden City.

> STOKER
> But they wouldn't have archived me, Maximos.
> (shakes his head, lips pursed, resolute)
> I can assure you there's no record
> of MY past in those Archives
> – I'm not royalty.

> MAXIMOS
> (his tone equally assertive)
> Not royalty, but highly significant:
> you're Kirk Jr's brother, who governed the
> city before it was destroyed by the bomb.

> STOKER
> Governor Kirk's HALF-
> brother. Who was white.

---

* Austin will often have this clipboard with him when he appears in Simian City scenes, on which he writes down Maximos' orders (it replaces the script he carries in the other scenes), just as his character Anderson did in ASSAULT.

                    (takes a slow breath, swallows)
                    D'you know what it says in the
                    column beneath "father" on
                    my birth certificate?

                              MAXIMOS
                    (pauses, considers this)
                    The name of Kirk Jr's father ...
                    who would also've been YOUR father.

        Austin takes out his billfold and removes a square of tightly-folded paper.
He opens it carefully into the long, narrow, tattered and browned certificate.
Through the worn paper we see traces of handwriting, mixed with print, an
official wine-colored wax seal at the back.

                              STOKER
                    Here, you read it.

        Stoker hands it over. Maximos' expression shows surprise.

                              MAXIMOS
                    You carry your
                    birth certificate with you?

                              STOKER
                    I do.

        Close-up of Maximos, carefully scrutinizing the ancient document. He
pronounces the syllables slowly.

                              MAXIMOS
                    Il-le-gitimate.

        Close-up of Austin, his jaw tightening, not quite a grimace.
Camera steps back.

                              MAXIMOS
                    Explain, Stoker.
                    The significance of your term.

                    (he hands back the certificate)

                         - here ...

36

Austin speaks distractedly, while he slowly and delicately refolds his
certificate.

                    STOKER
          My mother was black, Maximos,
          descendent of African slaves ...
          (returns the certificate to his bill-
          fold, still speaking absentmindedly)
          ... nothing but a third-class citizen.
          Worse: she was a nigger. Which makes
            ME a nigger ... even though
               my father was white,
               AND a Governor.

Suddenly Eva rushes over from the kitchen, brandishing her wooden spoon -
looking shocked, aghast. She stares at Austin.

                     EVA
                     NO!

He turns to her, momentarily confused.
After a resonant pause, Eva explains.

                     EVA
            You said the n-word,
          forbidden by Maximos since the
          founding of the Obomites a decade ago.
          (gestures forcefully with her spoon)
              Our First Commandment!

With her other hand Eva raises her medallion and respectfully kisses the
image.

Camera cuts to a close-up of Eva's hairy chimp-hand, her crimson-painted
fingernails, holding up the medallion: for the first time we see the Hanuman-
Obama portrait clearly.

Maximos speaks in a subdued tone, as Eva returns to the kitchen.

                   MAXIMOS
                 ... Lucky it's
          Maximos you're talking to.
          We'll grant absolution
                 ... this once.

                    STOKER
                  Thank you.
            I shouldn't've forgotten.

                   MAXIMOS
                (inquisitively)
        But tell me, Stoker, what do you
        mean by calling yourself ...
          that discriminatory term?
          It's generally - crudely -
              applied to others.

                    STOKER
          I AM your other, Maximos,
        any way you look at it. But it's
        not just a matter of appearances,
      not just a matter of power. I've had my
    history taken from me - severed, silenced.
    Not just my ancient history, but also my
      more recent, individual history ...
              (pauses, resigned)
          I'm illegitimate through-
                and-through.

                   MAXIMOS
                 (considers)
              Then you're no
            different from me.

                    STOKER
              (shakes his head)
            That's not quite accurate,
        Maximos. It's not true. You didn't
      know your parents because they were
      murdered when you were an infant.
      But we know them, history knows them,
      it's all in the records. Consequently,
      you know your place in the world.

                   MAXIMOS
                (assertively)
            That's why we're going
            in search of your tape.

                    STOKER
               As I was saying ...
          (shakes head vehemently again)
           I can assure you there're no
            tapes of illegitimate nig-
           BLACKS - in the Archives
             of Forbidden City.

                   MAXIMOS
              I beg to differ.

                    STOKER
              How so, Maximos?

                   MAXIMOS
        You're still Governor Kirk Jr's brother.
       Still your father's son. You carry his blood, his
        genes - despite your skin color. As such, you're
         still royalty, still highly significant ...
              (pauses, considers)
            most important of all -

                    STOKER
               Yes, Maximos?

                   MAXIMOS
              - you're the former
          Director of Security Operations.

Maximos pauses again, reflectively - suddenly distraught.

                   MAXIMOS
                  That is ...
            before the bomb dropped
           and eradicated it all ...
             (pauses dramatically)
                Civilization!
            - human and simian both.

There's a moment of weighty silence before Stoker speaks.

                    STOKER
              ... You were
             saying, Maximos?

He returns to the subject at hand.

                    MAXIMOS
          I was stating the obvious
          fact that, as the former Director of
          Security Operations, YOU know the physical
          layout of Forbidden City like it's ...
               (pauses, finding his words)
               like it's blueprinted on
               the back of your
               own memory.

Austin raises his brows, skeptical.

                    MAXIMOS
          What I'm trying to point out Stoker,
          is this: you're nothing but a walking
          security risk yourself.
          Which means —

                    STOKER
               (almost convinced)
          — there might be a tape of my
          history in those —

                    MAXIMOS
               (full smile)
          I'd wager on it!

Camera reverses abruptly to a shot exposing the crew and technicians, revealing that this is a set. On the other side of the treehouse, in their three tall canvass chairs, sit the Director, 2nd Director, and the Producer (still smoking his cigar).
          A female crewmember snaps a clapperboard before the camera while —

                    DIRECTOR
               Cut!
               (enthusiastically)
          That's a take!

5

Dissolve to an exterior shot of Maximos' treehouse, as seen from ground level. In the windows above we make out the cameras and technicians, still assembled. While below, off to the right side of the frame, Austin hurries discretely down the last steps of the bamboo ladder.
He hastens toward the Johnny-on-the-Spot.

Medium shot of Austin pushing in the door, "Johnny-on-the-Spot" stenciled on it in black spray paint.

The door opens into the Men's Room at StarBucks: we watch Austin rush toward the urinal, quickly pull the waist of his track pants down and spread his legs to pee. As the camera draws in on Austin's face - his cheeks puffed for a second as he tolerates the pain, then relaxes into a beatific expression. We continue watching his face as he shakes out the last drops.

Medium shot of Austin pulling in the Men's Room door, "M" inscribed on the other side.

The camera follows Austin, script folded under his arm, past a few tables with seated patrons. At their table Maximos is sitting alone (still in his chimp disguise). Now there's only the single script before him, which Maximos is reading, and a large paper cup of coffee. He looks up at Austin approaching, smiles.

                    MAXIMOS
                    Jesus-H!
                Took you a century
                  to get that out!

                    STOKER
              (raises eyebrows)
              Stings like a bitch.

Austin takes his seat facing Maximos.

                    STOKER
                - so where'd those
              other two goons go?

                    MAXIMOS
            They think they can get in nine
            holes before the next shoot.

                    STOKER
              (pages through his script)
           Rough life, being a star -

The attendant from the earlier scene arrives suddenly, holding a large
paper cup of coffee. He cuts Austin off, placing the cup down on the table before
him.

                    ATTENDANT
               Grande neegro,
               two EX shots.

He departs, same smug look on his face.
Austin grabs hold the the edges of the table with both hands, rising
slightly - ready to go after the boy - incensed. He takes a deep breath to calm
himself, sits again and releases hold of the table. He turns his attention back to
the script.

                    STOKER
               So . . .
              (finds his place)
               take it up where
               we left off?

                    MAXIMOS
               You got it.

Austin reads silently. He raises his coffee cup and swirls it a bit, sniffs
the aroma, slowly takes a sip - working the coffee back and forth between his
slightly puffed cheeks, considering.

                    STOKER
           Nice berry-plum flavor, touch of
           spice, soft generous finish . . .
               not bad at all, Maximos.

                    MAXIMOS
           Homer's vintage. He's become
           something of a connoisseur.

                    STOKER
           Is there anything Homer
               doesn't know about?

                    MAXIMOS
          He doesn't know your history, Stoker.
        That's why we're going to look for your tape
        in the Archives of Forbidden City. Same way
          you helped me find my tape ten years ago.

                    STOKER
              (warmed by the gesture)
              You'd do that for me?

                    MAXIMOS
          We orphans have to stick together!

                    STOKER
            (contemplates reflectively)
          I'm only a HALF-orphan, Maximos.
        It's only my father I don't know much about.
        Only saw him once, at four years of age ...
          My mother took me to meet him before he
            left Trinidad for New York City ...
            destination, Presbyterian Hospital:
                they removed a brain tumor,
                  but in those days ...

Austin shakes his head, stoical.

                    STOKER
              He never survived.
              Returned to the island
                in a box.

Brief pause. Maximos' tone is more encouraging.

                    MAXIMOS
              Yet you did see him.
              You did meet him.

                    STOKER
                    Once.

                    MAXIMOS
              And surely you heard
            about him from your mother.

STOKER
That's the thing ...
my mother was fiercely private,
she scarcely mentioned him.

MAXIMOS
Curious.

STOKER
As am I.

Austin puts his cup down and turns to Maximos – an earnest, searching
expression on his face.

STOKER
I want to know more, Maximos.
How did he meet my mother? What kind of
relationship did they have? And if he loved
my mother – as I believe she loved him – why does
it say "illegitimate" on my birth certificate?
(after a short pause)
Why didn't he claim me?

MAXIMOS
(raises his chin assertively)
The tape will tell us.

STOKER
(still doubtful)
But if those mutants in Forbidden City
continue to survive, then they're dangerous.
And the place still buzzes with radioactivity
– ever since the bomb destroyed it,
and drove 'em underground.

MAXIMOS
(still with his chin raised, still confident)
IF they survive ... but we made it into the
Archives once, for me, and WE survived.
Now, Stoker – mutants or not –
we'll return there for you.

We see that Austin is again genuinely moved.
Maximos smiles, letting down his guard; Austin slowly does the same.

                        MAXIMOS
                    Homer won't let
                us get into any trouble.

                        STOKER
                    (raises his cup)
                If we can keep him sober.

                        MAXIMOS
                  (raises his own cup)
                We'll just have to consume
                      his vintage −

                        STOKER
                    − before he does.

They touch cups, drink.

6

Cut to an exterior long shot from behind the faded black Toyota, at the side of Austin and Robin's home in Studio City. It's early evening, sky faintly pink in the background behind the red, barrel-tiled roof. On the left side of the frame we watch Austin lean his bicycle against the wall, then reach into the basket for his script.

Cut to an interior view of the small dining room/kitchen: all appears exactly as in the opening sequence, except now Robin (smartly dressed from work) and Austin are seated at the crudely-hewn table and stools from Maximos' treehouse, transposed to their Studio City home; it indicates that the scene takes place, to greater or lesser extent, in Austin's mind.

The camera draws in – they're eating Chinese food out of wire-handled, trapezoid-shaped cartons with chopsticks. There's a bottle of red wine on the table and two half-filled, stemmed glasses, in addition to other cartons of food, the wicker basket with bananas, and the prescription medicine vial.

Robin swallows, pinches up another mouthful of fried rice from her carton. She halts with her chopsticks raised half-way to her mouth.

"Well? Harry give you a part?"

Austin looks at her, also eating.

"Yeah ... pretty sure."

"As?"

Robin makes a swirling motion with her empty chopsticks, speeding him up. He holds up a pinched shrimp.

"A stud gorilla. Virile. With a sound memory ... " He swallows the shrimp, smiles.

"And a healthy prostate."

Robin thinks back to the film from forty-three years ago, tries to recall.

"Gabo?"

"He died in ASSAULT." After a pause Austin clarifies, "The SIMIAN one."

He continues.

"... Remember, after Gabo murdered his son Amadeus, Maximos tossed him out the tree?"

"I guess."

Austin pinches another mouthful, his tone serious.

"I'm playing a human – African American."

Robin tries to recall the film again.

"... Anderson? Wasn't that your character's name?"

He shakes his head, looks at her.

"Stoker," he says bluntly.

Her face is abruptly puzzled – like she hasn't heard him right.

"Who?" she asks cautiously.

"Stoker," he repeats. "I'm playing Stoker."

Robin holds up her empty chopsticks. She stares at him – surprisingly, complicatedly upset: frightened, frustrated, flabbergasted.

"Stoker?" she says. "How can you play Stoker?"

She takes a deep breath, tries to calm herself.

There's a brief, tense silence.

Suddenly Robin slams her chopsticks down – flat beneath her palm – a loud, smacking noise against the primitive wood table.

"Austin, you ARE Stoker."*

---

* POSTSCRIPT trailer: www.robertantoni/postscript

7

Cut to a close-up of Stoker's fist - pounding fiercely against a strongly fortified, crudely constructed plank door. Beside his fist is the rudimentary wrought-iron grille.

The camera pulls back to an exterior shot of the ARMORY in Simian City: it's late night/early morning. Homer and Maximos (both as apes) are seen from behind with their backs flanking Stoker's, the three of them standing before the Armory's door in the half-dark.

Austin speaks in a resigned tone.

> STOKER
> He's asleep.

> HOMER
> Not eternally,
> I trust.

> VESUVIUS
> (his ancient voice sounding
> from behind the door)
> Who knocks?

> STOKER
> Stoker.

A hinged sentry-hatch opens behind the grille, revealing the red and rheumy eyes of an aged orangutan.

> VESUVIUS
> And what does
> Stoker want?

> STOKER
> (vehemently)
> Weapons.

> VESUVIUS
> For what purpose?

Stoker nudges Homer into dialectic action. *

                    HOMER
                 We require them ...

Homer interrupts himself. He raises the Spanish leather bota hanging
around his neck and squeezes it - shooting a long, curved stream of red wine
expertly into his mouth. He bites off the stream, swallows.

                    HOMER
              ... for self-protection.
                 In the pursuit of
                   knowledge.

Homer wipes his mouth with the back of a hairy hand.

                   VESUVIUS
              Self-protection against
                 whom or what?

                    HOMER
              (raises ape eyebrows)
                 We're not sure.

                   VESUVIUS
            Then what is the purpose of protecting
            yourself against a danger of which you have
             no knowledge, in pursuit of a knowledge
                 you don't possess?

Stoker shakes his head, his tone frustrated, voice barely audible.

                   STOKER
                Jesus-fuckin'-H.

                   VESUVIUS
                  (oblivious)
                Is it knowledge
                for good or evil?

                    HOMER
             All knowledge is for good ...

---

* author disclaims the term "dialectic action" as somewhat overblown, but retains
it here to remain faithful to the script of the simian ASSAULT

He takes another quick shot from his bota.

                    HOMER
          ... only the use to which you put it
                can be good or evil.

                    MAXIMOS
            (also growing exasperated)
        The sun will rise in approximately
        three hours. I should like this matter
          to be settled before it sets.

                    VESUVIUS
              (vigorously protesting)
        Maximos appointed me not only as the
        keeper of this Armory, but also as the keeper
        of his own conscience. That's why I've asked
          six boring questions - and now propose to
          ask another - before issuing, or not
            issuing, the weapons you requested.

Vesuvius pauses; he clears his throat dramatically.

                    VESUVIUS
            What is the nature of this
            knowledge you cannot seek
                without weapons?

                    MAXIMOS
                    (hastily)
              The knowledge of
            Stoker's past. Recorded
          on a tape in the Archives
            of Forbidden City.

                    STOKER
                (adds quickly)
            Which is contaminated,
        but may still be inhabited by -

                    HOMER
                (cuts him off)
                - humans.

He pauses; clears his throat dramatically.

                    HOMER
          - white, mutant humans.

                   VESUVIUS
          (ape eyeballs open wide)
             The horror!*

He closes the small sentry-gate behind the crude grille.

                   VESUVIUS
                  Do come in.

Vesuvius unbolts and opens the heavy plank door as they enter. The Armory
appears just as Austin remembers it from the earlier simian film, with all manner
of dated and dusty weapons stacked, piled or crated along the walls. The room is
illuminated by burning oil in small bowls. Vesuvius speaks stalwartly, with a
comprehensive sweep of his ape arm.

                   VESUVIUS
          Take your protective pick.

                   MAXIMOS
             (equally stalwart)
          Three submachine guns.

                   VESUVIUS
              (distrustfully)
                    For?

Homer raises his bota in a toast.

                    HOMER
              The removal of
               testicles.**

Stoker looks sideways at Homer, raises his human eyebrows.

_____

* author references Marlow's description of Kurtz in Conrad's great African saga,
HEART OF DARKNESS
** this line and others in the scene are the author's admiring nod to the script of
ASSAULT, where Homer answers Vesuvius' question, "The removal of obstacles"

                    STOKER
                  Ammunition.

Vesuvius guides them from stash to stash. He speaks musingly.

                    VESUVIUS
          I don't really hold with knowing
          about the past - especially Stoker's
              (pauses, considers him)
          - which is undoubtedly dark.

                    HOMER
              And Ginger Schnapps.
              (smiles sarcastically)
            I mean a Geiger Counter.

                    VESUVIUS
          (oblivious, speaks ponderingly)
          ... I mean, if we knew for a fact there
          was an afterlife ... and the afterlife was
          bliss eternal, we'd all commit suicide
                in order to enjoy it.

Stoker shakes his head - profoundly frustrated, exasperated.

                    STOKER
                   Pistols.

                    VESUVIUS
                     For?

                    HOMER
            (after another quick shot)
          It's a dangerous journey. With
          Maximos' permission, Stoker may
             wish to shoot a number
               of Caucasians.

                    VESUVIUS
                  (fearfully)
              Better take three!

    He tosses each of them a Smith and Wesson; they take up holsters and strap
them on.
        Old Vesuvius considers his king respectfully.

VESUVIUS
Enjoy your ordeal.*

With a bow to Maximos, Vesuvius ceremoniously ushers our trio out the door.

Cut to an exterior shot of the Armory: Vesuvius stands in the open doorway, watching our trio depart in the near foreground. Maximos nods at him over his shoulder.

MAXIMOS
He may be old,
but he has a mind
like a sponge.**

HOMER
When I was a boy . . .

He interrupts himself – takes a long, arching shot from his bota, expertly bites off the stream.

HOMER
. . . he was my
teacher.***

We watch as our trio starts off on their adventure, submachine guns slung officially over their shoulders, pistols holstered, carrying their various equipment.

---

* "meal" in ASSAULT
** "razor"   "   "

*** Homer: www. robertantoni.com/homer

8

Cut to an interior shot of the table at StarBucks: Austin is seated in the middle
with Homer to one side (now as an older gentleman), and Maximos (also without his
ape disguise) sitting at the other. All are dressed in their civvies.

Unlike all of the other actors, however, Maximos appears perfectly preserved
– flawlessly unaged – exactly as Austin remembers him forty-three years ago –

*

There are scripts open on the table before them, and large paper cups of
coffee. Stoker raises his palm to shade his brow against the fierce glare.

                    STOKER
               Look, gentlemen . . .
               the sun's rising.

                    MAXIMOS
          How long've we been trudging
          through this vile desert?

                    STOKER
          (checks his wristwatch)
          Almost three hours.

* Maximos: www. robertantoni.com/maximos

                         MAXIMOS
                      And no sight of
                    Forbidden City yet?

                          STOKER
              (he peers off into the distance)
                 Nothing, Maximos. Only desert
                     - this barren wasteland
                        left by the bomb.

                         MAXIMOS
                      (skeptically)
                 You sure we're walking
               in the right direction, Homer?

     Homer takes a drink from his cup, then removes from his pocket his -
imaginary - compass. He peers at it.

                          HOMER
                        Oh, dear.
                    Seems we've veered
                   slightly off course.
                   By approximately ...
                     (he studies it)
                      180 degrees.

                          STOKER
                    (shakes his head)
                 You're holding your compass
                    upside-down, Homer.

                          HOMER
                 (turns his compass around)
                     Ah! There we go,
                       right on course.

     Maximos, exhausted, mops his brow with a paper napkin.

                         MAXIMOS
              The heat shall be upon us presently.
               How much water have you left
                    in your canteen, Stoker?

                    HOMER
               (offers his cup)
              Care for a shot of
             grape juice, Maximos?

                   MAXIMOS
          I think not. And if you don't
        behave yourself old-man, we're going
         to confiscate your submachine gun.

                    STOKER
           (hands over his own cup)
           Here Maximos, take a drink.

                   MAXIMOS
               (drinks heartily)
                Much obliged!

                    HOMER
          Barring miscalculations, I should
          guestimate that any moment now –

Stoker interrupts, points off into the distance.

                    STOKER
            There it is, gentlemen . . .
                Forbidden City!

                   MAXIMOS
           (shades his brow, aghast)
                Exactly as it was
                 a decade ago.

                    HOMER
          (shades his brow as well)
              Like a storm at sea,
                   but . . .
                 solidified.

                    STOKER
            A veritable hell-hole
                . . . Hades.

                    MAXIMOS
                 (dramatically)
              It's where we're headed.*

    As the scene ends Stoker is caught up in a vivid and intense moment of déjà
vu: suddenly it's as though he's back on the set with his companions, forty-three
years ago.
    Pleasantly confused, with a half-smile, he turns from the desert vista
stretching out before him and looks squarely into the camera, vaguely hoping to
locate himself.

* Maximos' Home Videos: www.robertantoni.com/maximoshomevideos

9

Cut to a reverse panoramic shot of FORBIDDEN CITY, completely destroyed by the H-bomb: the charred remains of a lost civilization rise ominously out of the horizon in the distance, desert filling the lower half of the frame. "It symbolizes the total desolation of one of man's great cities – New York? – massive, silent, utterly dead. A monument to all twisted and contradictory ideas and passions that drove man to suicide."*

The camera switches to a long shot of our trio (Maximos transformed to chimpanzee, Homer to orangutan), as we watch them trudge with difficulty up a steep sandbank toward the city gates – lugging their submachine guns and various equipment.

Cut to a shot within the demolished city (back-lot tank at MGM Studios). We watch our trio forage among the debris, slowly making their way. The city was not so much exploded apart, as melted into solidity by the enormous temperatures at the center of the H-bomb. Forbidden City appears exactly as Austin recalls it from the 1973 film: a low-tech, low-budget, dated-looking depiction of the H-bomb's destruct-tion of a modern city – creative and inventive, yet on closer inspection, not much more sophisticated than the set of a high school play.

Our trio lumbers cautiously past a school bus that appears half-melted into the side of a former steel-and-glass skyscraper. Austin, ahead, comes to a halt in the middle of the street. He peers up at the twisted tower before him, turning back his mind.

                    STOKER
          25th Street and 6th Avenue:
        I once lived in this building on the
        seventh floor, in the apartment above my
        brother's – looks like the third floor now.

Austin pauses, considering. He points his submachine gun down at the manhole cover beneath his feet.

                    STOKER
              If I remember correctly,
         the Emergency Exit for the Archives
        should be located somewhere below here
            – their way OUT is our way IN.

Homer – wearing an old-fashioned, bulky-looking headset over his ape ears – studies his Geiger Counter. He looks alarmed as the clicks speed up (we also hear them on the sound track, see the meter's needle jumping erratically).

_____
* particularly eloquent description from script of ASSAULT

                    HOMER
              Well, you better
          get us in there quick -

                   MAXIMOS
              (equally alarmed)
              - and out. Before
              the radiation melts
          US like everything else!

     We hear a loud crash as Stoker flips over the heavy iron manhole cover.
Abruptly, with the noise, the melted half-school bus to our left comes to life - its
red lights blinking. We see the stop sign extend, and the school hand-bell we heard
earlier in the opening sequence begins ringing from an unseen source.
     Our trio, startled, stare over at the bus. Stoker's tone is anxious - yet
measured, professional.

                   STOKER
              Looks like somebody
              spotted us. Quick
              - down here!

     He leads Maximos and Homer down the manhole.

     Cut to an interior shot of our trio, brandishing their submachine guns
protectively, hurrying cautiously along a subterranean sewer tunnel. Pipes
and wires hang all about, walls filthy, mud dripping. The school bell is slowly
diminished as they continue, Maximos and Homer following Stoker along a tunnel
that opens up into a small rock-and-steel-walled cavern, with two other tunnels
branching out.
     They pause, looking around, unsure.

     Maximos raises his submachine gun - slowly, tremulously - pointing it up at
a security camera high on opposite wall.

                   MAXIMOS
                    It...
                    moved.

     Switch to a close-up of the dusty and dated-looking security camera. After
a second we see a small red light beneath the lens blink slowly - and the camera
begins to pan, sluggishly, making a low, grinding noise.

     Reverse shot of our trio, brandishing their submachine guns, staring up at
the security camera high on the wall.

STOKER
We better get going!

Maximos and Homer follow him into one of the tunnels.

10

Cut to a medium shot of three dusty, dented, gray-metal bomb canisters. The tallest one stands in the center, flanked by the two shorter bombs, cavernous rock wall rising behind. Hanging around the necks of each of these bombs are gaudy chains holding framed and glass-covered photograph portraits – we can't make them out yet – like overgrown religious scapulars. Beneath the central bomb's scapular, in stenciled black spray paint, "DRUMPF II" is inscribed; on the smaller bomb to our left, "DRUMPF I"; and the smallest bomb to our right, "JR".

The camera steps back to reveal the cavernous underground CHAPEL of Forbidden City. We see dusty wooden benches, with kneelers, assembled in a semi-circle before the crude stone altar supporting the three scapulared bombs. A handful of parishioners kneel or sit, quietly praying; an older woman fingers rosary beads suspended from her hand. To one side of the altar is a wrought-iron stand with multiple artificial candles flickering, a slot for 25¢ coins to be inserted.

All of the inhabitants of Forbidden City are white humans; all zealously self-identify as whites. They are middle-class, "American-looking", with no visible traces of other ethnicities. Unlike the inhabitants of Forbidden City in the previous ASSAULT film, there are no blacks, no multiracial, non-white humans. All show signs of radiation damage – raised scars on their exposed skin, dark splotches. In addition, all of the white inhabitants of Forbidden City in POSTSCRIPT, including the youngest children, wear red baseball caps – like fraternity or sorority caps – with the Greek letters "Tau-Rho" inscribed in white on the front of their caps over their foreheads. None of them wear their baseball caps turned backward.

A young mother kneels alongside her three children. She crosses herself and kisses her thumb and forefinger, stands, ushers her children out.

The camera draws in closer on the three bombs: it finally reveals to us that the picture-portrait on the scapular of the largest, central bomb is that of Donald J Drumpf; the middle-sized bomb to our left, Frederick Christ Drumpf; and the smallest bomb to our right, Donald "Jr" Drumpf.*

---

* Historians will recall that by his first presidential mandate, Donald J Trump, son of Frederick Christ Trump, reinstated his family surname with the ancestral Germanic "Drumpf," thus evading all alleged conflict-of-interest charges with his Real Estate Company and Brand. By this shrewd legal maneuver he also successfully negated his still unreleased, and outstanding, back taxes worth – according to one boastful presidential tweet – "many many millions."

Camera steps back to a long shot revealing, at the rear of the Chapel, the glassed-off wall of Forbidden City's CENTRAL CONTROL, security personal assembled inside.

Switch to a shot within Central Control: the camera pans, showing the security personnel and technicians, male and female, seated at long tables studying dated-looking black-and-white television monitors. In the background, through the three large pane-glass windows, we see the Chapel with its scapulared bombs and praying parishioners. The security personnel and technicians all wear nondescript uniforms of black turtlenecks and coarse black trousers, with the red baseball caps. Beside an ancient microwave in the back of the room are a number of stacked, rusty, vintage cans - Spaghetti-O's, Chef Boyardee Raviolis, Spam, Miniature Franks - some of the cans left open, their cut scalloped-tops backfolded, in addition to plastic utensils and used paper plates with discarded food. Among the documents and paraphernalia scattered on the tables, the discarded food on paper plates, we make out a number of vintage IHA* beer cans, some crushed; and a few gumbo-sized plastic beer steins with an inch or two of brown liquid and leftover lemon slices sunk to the bottom.

Cut to a shot looking down over the shoulder of one of the male technicians. On his monitor we see a partially destroyed, above-ground bodega, in the process of being pillaged by several scavengers. In addition to their black uniforms and caps, the scavengers wear khaki military-style backpacks and old-fashioned motorcycle goggles, some brandishing crowbars.

Cut to a close-up of a dust-covered scavenger. He stands before a wall of dusty liquor bottles - tequila, vodka, white rum, gin, triple sec. The scavenger talks into a bulky and dated-looking walky-talky, but the voice on the sound track is scratchy, as though were hearing it in the Central Control room.

SCAVENGER
Scavenger 4 to
Central Control...

Return to the shot over the technician's shoulder. He talks into a large and dated-looking microphone on the table beside his monitor, ransacked bodega and scavenger appearing on the screen before him.

MALE TECHNICIAN
(speaks officially)
Go ahead, Scavenger 4...

----

* Native American lager brewed in Buffalo, NY: Indian Head Ale (Iroquois tribe, pictured on can)

we've successfully activated and
tapped into the emporium's security camera.

On his screen we see the dust-covered scavenger, speaking into his walky-talky, liquor bottles rising behind.

                    SCAVENGER
          (scratchy voice - smiling, excited)
        Found us a damn treasure trove up here, Fred!
          Like we got every ingredient,
                 even the sec!

                 MALE TECHNICIAN
             (letting down his guard)
         Whoo-daddy! Fredrick-fuckin'-H!
         Get that shit home, Bob! Gonna have
            us a revival meetin' tonight!

                    SCAVENGER
            (on the screen, smiling - his
          voice scratchy, very excited)
               Long Island variety!

He points at the "TP" initials on his dusty cap with his free hand.

                    SCAVENGER
                They don't call us
             Tea Partiers for nothin'!

Cut to a shot of our trio - hurrying cautiously along a tunnel, following Stoker's lead. After a short while the tunnel opens up into a much larger steel-and-rock-walled cavern, this one with several tunnels branching out.
They halt, looking around, now thoroughly confused.
Maximos, out of breath, slowly points his submachine gun up at another security camera high on the opposite wall.

                     MAXIMOS
              (panting, frightened)
                   Look . . .
                 another one!

Our trio stare up at the security camera, its red light slowly blinking, as the camera pans sluggishly.

Cut to close-up of a female technician in Central Control. She stares alarmed into her monitor showing the empty cavern, talking loudly into her microphone.

FEMALE TECHNICIAN
Security breach! Security breach!
All available soldiers to Southwest Sector
– 25th Street and 6th Avenue!

We watch the female technician as GOVERNOR RUBIN and GENERAL KOCH* hurry over, concern visible on their faces. Rubin stands behind the technician, with Koch standing slightly behind him – all studying the monitor. Rubin and Koch wear the same uniform and cap, Koch with the addition of an unbuttoned camouflaged army vest.

RUBIN
(puzzled)
What . . .
is it?

Shot of the monitor: on the screen we see the camera slowly panning the empty subterranean cavern, its various tunnels branching off.
Return to the close-up of the female technician, studying her monitor, working the toggle on her desk – as we see the camera continue to pan the empty cavern on the screen before her.

FEMALE TECHNICIAN
(sounds perplexed, anxious)
Thought I saw something a minute
ago, Governor. But I wasn't sure . . .
I just saw it again!

RUBIN
(apprehensively)
What?

---

* Since the war between the mutants and the apes in the earlier film, resulting in the death of Governor Koch, Forbidden City has been governed by the benevolent Rubin, who has ensured that there be no further aggression directed toward the inhabitants of Simian City. For the past ten years there have been no interactions of any kind between the apes and the mutants – a decade of peace. In the blindness of his generosity, however, Rubin has made the egregious error of appointing Koch's younger brother – two peas of a pod – as his military General (his surname actually appears as "Kolp" in the script of the previous ASSAULT, indicating either a misspelling, or one of the author's clumsier attempts at parody).

Shot of the monitor: on the screen we see our trio come slowly, fuzzily into view, brandishing their submachine guns and staring up into the camera.

> FEMALE TECHNICIAN
> (offstage, as she
> slowly makes them out)
> Looks like . . .
> two apes and . . .

Cut back to close-up of the female technician studying her monitor, with Rubin and Koch standing just behind her – our trio visible on the screen before them, brandishing their submachine guns, looking up into the camera.

> KOCH
> (under his breath,
> but still audible)
> – and a God-dammed
> nigger.

> RUBIN
> Silence, Koch!
> We heard what you said . . .
> (suddenly very upset)
> And I won't tolerate that
> discriminatory explica-

> KOCH
> (cuts him off)
> Tolerate this,
> Rubin!

He withdraws a pistol from the leather holster under his vest and shoots Rubin in the back. Rubin slumps to floor.

> KOCH
> (to technician)
> Out of my way, missy!
> I'm runnin' the show now.

Koch shoves the female technician aside and takes her seat, gesturing backward over his shoulder.

> KOCH
> Been waitin' too long to get
> ridda that yellowbelly.

He aggressively clicks the toggle, shouting into the microphone.

                              KOCH
                    All available Soldiers!
                     Mobilize! Mobilize!

Cut to a shot of the monitor screen over Koch's shoulder: the image of our trio goes white and shifts fuzzily to a view of the subterranean ARMY GARRISON.

The camera pulls into the screen, transitioning to a panoramic shot of the underground garrison: we see male and female soldiers in their black uniforms and caps, all wearing camouflaged vests like Koch. All busy – inspecting, cleaning, repairing their guns – all manner of dated and dusty military equipment. There's an old tank, a couple of jeeps and, in the background to the rear of the garrison, an ancient and dust-covered school bus, its red lights blinking.

We suddenly hear the school bell ringing through a loudspeaker, as well as Koch's voice – shouting over the bell through the echoey loudspeaker.

                              KOCH
                    (offstage, his voice
                 reverberating dramatically)
                    All available soldiers!
                 Mobilize! Mobilize! 25th Street
                 and 6th Avenue – suspects have
                   entered underground sewer!

When the soldiers hear his instructions they jump up, grab their submachine guns, and begin filing out of the frame to our left.

Return to the close-up of Koch shouting into his microphone, the garrison and soldiers showing on the monitor before him. Other personnel are gathered at Koch's back, all looking concerned.

                              KOCH
                 I want 'em surrounded! I want
                 soldiers down the manhole at 25th,
                   more soldiers cutting 'em off at
                   all the underground tunnels!

He clicks his toggle aggressively, and the screen's picture returns to our trio – still staring up into the camera, still confused, their submachine guns raised. Now Koch speaks in a subdued tone to the technicians gathered behind him, as he points out the figures on his monitor screen.

                              KOCH
                        That's Maximos,
                       other ape's Homer
                        ... and the nig-
                     (halts, takes a breath)
                   the HUMAN'S name is Stoker,
                 Governor Kirk Jr's HALF-brother.
                 Used to run Security, back before the bomb.
                  Those three returned here a decade ago,
                 lookin' for Maximos' tape in the Archives.
                     (pauses for a breath)
                    That's how the WAR started.
                      Cause my brother ...
                        let 'em get away.

Close-up of Koch's face.

                              KOCH
                         - I'm not makin'
                          that mistake!

Cut to the previous shot of our trio, still stalled in the underground
cavern; still staring up at the security camera high on the wall, its small red
light slowly blinking.

       Return to Koch, with the image of our trio on his monitor. He looks over his
shoulder at the technicians behind him - raising his fist, shouting at them.

                              KOCH
                    Will somebody sound the
                    fuckin' alarm over there?!

Cut back to our trio, staring up at the security camera. Suddenly the school
bell begins ringing from an unseen source, though considerably louder.

                            MAXIMOS
                     (shouts over the bell)
                    It appears our mutant friends
                      are more alive than ever.

                            STOKER
                        And they've
                    definitely spotted us.

                              HOMER
                            (smiling)
                          Let's put a stop
                         to that, shall we?

        He raises his submachine gun and holds it against his hip, firing a volley
at the security camera – we watch the blasts of fire at the end of his gun's barrel,
as the camera disintegrates off the wall.

        Return to Koch and technicians, staring into the monitor before them. We
see Homer fire up into the camera, his submachine gun blasting, as the screen goes
fuzzily white.

                              KOCH
                              Shit!
                           We lost 'em!

        Here the camera gives us a quick, dramatic montage, with the school bell
ringing throughout:

        1) Soldiers hurry along a sewer tunnel, brandishing submachine guns.

        2) Soldiers file down a sewer hole, also brandishing submachine guns.

        3) Close-up shot tracking a male soldier – the Commander – hurrying along a
tunnel, shouting into his bulky walky-talky.

                           COMMANDER
                        (flustered, winded)
                         Where d'you think
                       they're headed, General?

        Return to Koch and technicians – on the monitor before them we see a close-
up of the Commander hurrying along the tunnel, speaking into his walky-talky.

                              KOCH
                    (loudly into his microphone)
                     Pretty sure it's the Archives.
                        Couple levels down –
                        (pauses, hesitant)
                       if I remember right.

COMMANDER
(on the monitor - he halts and turns
toward the camera, his voice scratchy)
But nobody's been down there
in years, General!

KOCH
(into his microphone)
Just find 'em! I want
the apes apprehended for
questioning. The nig-
(takes a breath)
- human I want shot!

Return to our trio, still halted in the underground cavern. Two soldiers
enter through the tunnel to our right, brandishing their submachine guns.
Homer, holding his submachine gun against his hip, fires a volley at the
soldiers entering. We watch them slump to the ground, one soldier managing to get
a few shots off, ricocheting off the ceiling and a metal pipe.
Maximos ducks his head dramatically. He nods at Homer as he speaks to
Stoker.

MAXIMOS
Seems the grape juice
has him a bit jumpy.

STOKER
(urgently, competently)
The Archives are this way,
two levels down.
Now I'm sure.

He leads Maximos and Homer into one of the tunnels.

Cut to a shot of Stoker, standing above a hatch in the floor of one of the
tunnels, pointing his submachine gun at it.

STOKER
Down here!

Stoker throws open the hatch and leads the other two down the ladder. As
Homer descends, he pulls the metal hatch closed behind him.

The camera gives us another quick, dramatic montage, with the school bell
again ringing throughout·

1) Close-up of Homer's ape hand as he turns the lever on the closed hatch, securing it from the inside.

2) Soldiers file down the manhole at 25th Street.

3) Solders enter the large underground cavern, stepping over the two dead soldiers at the entrance.

Camera draws in on the Commander, still flustered, as he surveys the several tunnels leading out from the cavern - shouting into his walky-talky.

> COMMANDER
> We lost 'em, General!
> Which way's the Archives?

Return to our trio - following Stoker's lead along a sewer tunnel. He halts and points his submachine gun at another hatch.

> STOKER
> Down here!

Return to Koch, shouting into his microphone, technicians gathered behind him. All study the monitor showing the Commander paused in the tunnel - looking lost, totally confused.

> KOCH
> DOWN! There has to
> be a way down! FIND IT!
> Don't let those God-damned
> sodomites get away!

Cut to Stoker, finally leading Maximos and Homer into the darkened subterranean ARCHIVES. The school bell goes silent as Homer closes and secures the metal emergency exit door; and as Stoker flips up a wall-switch illuminating a bank of dimly-flickering florescent overheads, covered by a special protective brown Mylar. In the Archives are multiple steel shelves, stacked top-to-bottom with labeled, dusty, gray-metal film canisters. All jumbled and disheveled.
We watch our trio searching anxiously through the canisters - pulling one out, checking the label, shoving it back in.

Here the camera switches to fast motion, indicating the passage of several frustrating, perilous minutes: it shows our trio searching eagerly through the canisters. Maximos appears for an instant bending over to grab a canister in the foreground to our right; replaced by Stoker reaching for a canister on the top shelf; then Homer appears for an instant standing on a stool in the left foreground, etc.

The camera returns to standard speed. It shows our trio, fatigued and deeply
frustrated, still searching through the tumbled canisters.
Stoker shakes his head, utterly resigned.

                    STOKER
              Didn't I tell you?
              ... no way MY history's
              archived in this place!

                    MAXIMOS
                 (also resigned)
              I hate to admit –

Homer cuts him off.

                    HOMER
              Hold on a moment,
                 gentlemen ...

He turns to Stoker – ponderingly, as though he's just experienced a profound
revelation.

                    HOMER
              What d'you say we take a look
              behind your father's back?

Stoker screws up his face at Homer like he's lost his marbles.

Smiling confidently, Homer carries his stool across the room to a large,
framed, black-and-white photograph portrait. The glass once covering it has
broken away, except for a single fragment remaining in a lower corner. The
portrait hangs by a rusted wire, askew on the wall to our right. The camera pulls
in. On a tarnished plaque screwed to the bottom of the picture frame we slowly
make out: GOVERNER KIRK SR.
        A graffiti artist has defamed the stalwart-looking gentleman – dressed in
military garb with a chest full of ribbons and medals pinned to his jacket – by
penciling on elaborate mustaches: they spiral round and round over both of the
governor's red, puffy cheeks.
        Homer climbs up onto his stool and takes down the portrait – exposing the
door of a rusted, gray-metal strongbox, embedded securely into the rock wall. In
the center of the door is the black disk circled by its white numbers and hash
marks. On the wall above the safe, the graffiti artist has penciled: BLUEBLOODS.
        Homer looks proudly over his shoulder.

                    HOMER
              Now, Señor Stoker . . .
             what's the combination?

     Stoker shakes his head, confounded. He nods at the portrait, which Homer
still holds in his hands.

                    STOKER
                 No idea . . .
              I don't even remember
                that dude's picture.

     Homer sighs and climbs down from the stool. He leans the portrait against
the wall and shrugs off his backpack, removing his old-fashioned Geiger Counter.

                    HOMER
               That "dude" happens
                to be your father.

     He fits the old-fashioned headphones over his ape ears, and unplugs them
from the Geiger Counter.

                    HOMER
              Seems this predicament
             calls for desperate measures.

     He climbs back up onto his stool.
     Remarkably, there's a jack located below the black disk on the strongbox
door, with a three-way toggle beside it labeled AM/FM/S-Box. Homer clicks the
toggle to the third position, plugs in his headphones. He slowly, painstakingly
turns the dial back and forth, clockwise and counter-clockwise (we hear the slow
clicks over the sound track).
     Stoker and Maximos take their places behind him, looking on anxiously; and
after a few tense moments, the door pops open. Homer is elated.

                    HOMER
                Most excellent.

     He pushes the door open completely, revealing a crooked stack of still more
gray-metal film canisters. Homer peers in, pulls one out.

                    HOMER
                  (delighted)
                I found it.

Cut to a close-up of the metal canister held in Homer's hairy ape-hand, and for the first time we notice the clunky-looking, gold Harvard University ring worn on his pointer finger. He turns the canister slowly as we read, inscribed around the canister's edge:

"ARCHIVAL REC. #7596663 - AUSTIN STOKER - SON OF GOVERNOR KIRK SR."

Cut to a medium shot of Stoker, examining a three-foot-length of the film he has unwound from the spool. He looks up.

> STOKER
> You found it, alright.

He turns toward an old, dusty machine sitting on the counter before him, as the camera pulls back.

> STOKER
> If I recall correctly . . .
> (behind him Homer raises ape eyebrows)
> The tape goes in here.
> And the picture should appear . . .
> on that monitor over there.

The camera follows his gesture, shifting toward the monitor and pulling into the screen. And after a moment the monitor comes to life, going from black to fuzzy white - as the picture flickers into view.

PORT-OF-SPAIN, TRINIDAD; BLACK-AND-WHITE OLD FILM LOOK

The sequence opens with a long interior shot of the dining room in a palatial, conspicuously wealthy French Colonial home: a formal dinner party is in progress.

The camera slowly draws in, roams the table and diners. The table is elaborately set with a white lace tablecloth and shining silverware, fine china with all manner of enticing West Indian food, cut-crystal glasses with champagne, red wine - a feast. The female diners wear elegant, white lace gowns, the men black tuxedos. At one end of the long table sits an older gentleman, of Corsican heritage, small in stature, with shaggy, graying mustaches; at the other end the somewhat younger, slightly plump "Madam" - of Spanish background. The other diners' backgrounds are Corsican, French, Spanish, Venezuelan - all white Creoles.

On the sound track we hear, over the clatter of eating and drinking, Trinidadian vernacular English - but also snippets of Spanish and French. Black female servants, in black uniforms with starched white bib aprons and head-caps, circulate discretely, serving food. A tuxedoed butler wearing white gloves carefully pours red wine.

Superimpose card over tablecloth in lower center of frame:

ARCHIVAL REC.
#7596663
AUSTIN STOKER
b. PORT OF SPAIN,
TRINIDAD, B.W.I.
11/7/1932

Card fades, as the camera continues to roam the table and diners.

TITLES BEGIN (Trinidad story)

*   *   *

II

THE MOVIE

1

I was sixteen when my ninety-seven-year-old grandmother pulled me toward her in her wheelchair, sitting beside her "vitrina" crowded with miniature plaster saints, curled photographs of dead relatives – her clear-plastic bottle shaped like the Virgin with its screw-off crown, half-filled with yellowed Lourdes Water she liked to sip from occasionally – a mischievous smile pulling across her vein-colored gums (she only wore her "pearls" – her false teeth – for company), whispering:

"Bobby, one thin' I could tell you about you grandfather – that man could fuck like hell."

It must have been true.

Barto died at the age of forty-nine, yet he left my grandmother with six boys and two girls, and another boy had died in infancy. That's one child for every 2.3 years of marriage. My grandmother used to say that by the time my father, their youngest, arrived – and she went into labor in the middle of a Christmas fête – she simply put her glass of ponche-crema down and climbed the stairs to look for a bed. And she never even bothered to take off her stockings. Then she went back down and danced to the parang.

Barto also had a mistress for several years, a woman born in Buenos Aires – supposedly of "aristocratic" blood – and supposedly he had three other children by this mistress. My grandmother told me she used to get together with her sometimes for lunch, both before and after Barto's death. They were friends. She made empanadas, my grandmother made pastelles. They spoke Spanish together: my grandmother was born in Venezuela, though she was sent to a convent-school in Trinidad as a young girl to learn English. I think my grandmother may have actually felt grateful to this Argentinian mistress; she saved her from three more children she'd have probably had to bear herself.

But I don't think my grandmother ever met Madeleine, Austin's mother. If she had, I like to believe my grandmother would have made friends with her, also. I like to imagine them having lunch and speaking Spanish together. I see them eating callaloo.

There aren't many photographs of Barto, though my grandmother did pass one down to us of the "famous" Salvatori wedding, in which she is a bridesmaid and Barto a groomsman - the wedding ceremony where Barto and my grandmother first met. Which is the reason they're not standing together in the picture, taken in the side grotto of the newly-constructed Salvatori home, "Mille fleurs".

My grandmother's handwriting can be seen in the upper right corner identifying everybody. The little groom in the middle is Joseph Salvatori, a Corsican who sold bolts of cloth off the back of his bicycle when he arrived in Trinidad. But he soon became wealthy, eventually constructing what is known as the Salvatori Building on Fredrick Street, a landmark, to house his department store. For years it remained the tallest building on the island. His bride is of Spanish background born in Trinidad. She couldn't speak French - at least not "proper" French - the language of her Corsican groom. And of course she couldn't understand his Corsican vernacular either. So, like many such couples in Trinidad in those early days who spoke different languages, they communicated in the language of their adopted colony, "improper" English.

My grandmother is head bridesmaid, second woman from the right – she boasted that her hat was the biggest of them all, but it's hard to tell – her arm entwined with that a prominent English surgeon. According to my grandmother he proposed to her multiple times, including on the day of the photograph. Yet he lived his life out as a bachelor. And when Barto died the surgeon proposed to her one last time, twenty-three years after the photograph was taken.

I don't have to tell you who Barto is, cigar poised between his fingers like he's got more important things to think about. He's really incidental to the wedding ceremony itself, yet the entire photograph is somehow about him. Somehow he manages to eclipse them all, to dwarf them all, even my grandmother. Even the unfortunate surgeon trying his best to stand up tall. And YOU can tell me if the woman clasping his arm is smiling saucily, scared out of her skin, or both.

Bartolomeo Odillo Antoni was born in Corsica, but he immigrated as a young man to Trinidad. He became a successful trader of coffee, cocoa, and primarily tonka beans, produce of the island, some grown on his own small estate in Chaguaramas.*

The Salvatori wedding photograph is prophetic in that it marks not only the meeting of my grandparents, but years later my grandmother would successfully plot the marriage of her daughter, Carmen, to the Salvatoris' only son, Henry – who'd turn out even shorter, and became even wealthier, than his father. But I've decided that this photograph is prophetic for another reason, and for another person not seen in it. She wouldn't even have been hidden away in the kitchen of the newly-built French Colonial home, where they're gathered in the side grotto for the wedding photograph.

Not yet.

The Salvatori newlyweds would eventually hire a young black Creole girl by the name of Madeleine Stoker, of African and Portuguese background, as their house and kitchen servant. Madeleine was born on the smaller and poorer French

---

* This estate was eventually expropriated from my grandmother (after Barto's death) by the British and turned over to the Americans in a "Lend-Lease Treaty" to build their Military Base, which thrived on the island during WWII. The estate features prominently in Robert Antoni's story collection MY GRANDMOTHER'S EROTIC FOLK-TALES.

Antillean island of Guadeloupe; but she was taken by her parents at a young age first to Caracas, where she also learned Spanish, then to settle in Trinidad. The same Spanish she would speak with Madam Salvatori. Madeleine soon became her madam's favorite.

If this were an actual film – "flim" as we say in Trinidad – then the imagined scene of the dinner party we have begun to witness would have taken place inside the same home that forms the background of the photograph, only the dinner would occur nineteen years later. After the Salvatoris had been married for nineteen years – and my grandparents had been married for nineteen years – and my father, their youngest, had been born and reached the age of three. Barto died before my father turned eight.

Austin, born the year after the imagined dinner party – 1932 – would, at Barto's death, have reached the age of four.

Returning to the dinner where we left it, we see through the camera's eye as it roams the table and diners, giving us all the particulars of this West Indian setting, this historical moment – all of the food, dress, "culture" – the ostentatiousness of these white Creole diners, in stark contrast to the blacks serving them. That impassable gulf.

The scene is emblematic.

Now the camera slowly narrows its focus, bringing us back to our story, this story: it settles on Barto. More than that, the camera now feels glued to him. As though it can't shift from his figure: his jet black, slicked-back hair. Porcelain skin. His flashing eyes. Lush lashes. Elaborate mustache. His masculine hands with the manicured nails. The conviction of every gesture.

The camera pulls back, widening its gaze, but still centered on Barto, still glued to Barto. Suddenly, as though stepping forth from a blurred background, one of the servants comes sharply into focus. She's working her way around the table, corving white rice from a silver platter. Her movements are dexterous, firm, dignified – almost haughty: a French Creole, early twenties, her skin a rich burnt-sienna, long hair in a single braid wound into a crown beneath her cap. Her striking feature is her large, glossy, almond-shaped eyes.

We watch as she works her way around the table. Diner by diner, plate by plate. Eventually, she comes to Barto, reaching slightly over his shoulder to serve him. We see his head shift, inattentive at first – looking slightly back, slightly up.

Then the camera does that magical thing that astonishes and perplexes language. That outperforms language. That magical thing that only a camera can do: it gives us a moment, isolated within the continuum of time. No one but us sees it – fleeting, unspoken, irrefutable: the sudden electricity that passes between Barto and Madeleine. When their eyes lock for an instant.

Suddenly Madeleine cannot continue around the table. We watch her pause, distracted, and she turns her head and looks straight at us – her witness, implicated. As we watch her raise her right hand still holding the silver spoon to her forehead briefly – a single grain of white rice, as if in slow motion, falls from spoon to platter again – and she turns and walks brusquely out of the frame to our left.

*   *   *

INTERMISSION

1

Open with an interior shot of the underground Archives: from behind, we look over Austin's shoulder, the monitor before him still showing the dinner scene in progress.
    We watch the monitor's screen for a few seconds.

    Suddenly, off to our right, behind the offstage emergency exit door through which our trio had entered earlier, we hear a loud commotion - pounding, shouting.

    The camera steps back to reveal Maximos' and Homer's backs behind Stoker's, the three of them turning together from the monitor to look toward the door.

2

The camera also shifts to a shot of the door, with its unilluminated emergency exit sign above - as Maximos and Homer rush into the frame to begin piling up desks and chairs before the door, barricading it from the inside.
    We watch for a minute as they continue mounting up the desks and chairs.

3

Return to the shot of the monitor over Austin's shoulder: the picture on the screen having shifted from the extravagant dinner scene, to the kitchen of the palatial West Indian home.
    Slowly pulling in.

*   *   *

The kitchen is chaotic. A servant enters grasping an empty porcelain platter in each hand. She stoops to put them down atop the stack on the floor beside a barebacked boy who is washing dishes in a large wooden bucket overflowing with suds. The tuxedoed black butler, wearing white gloves, his face concentrated and shining with perspiration, hurries out with another freshly uncorked bottle of red wine in one hand, bottle of champagne trailing a faint line of vapor in the other. Another servant carries a platter covered with slices of imported Dutch Edam cheese: large half-disks, wedged, their semi-circular skins of bright crimson wax hugging the outer curves. Another servant exits with a cut-crystal bowl of Catalan membrillo.

A whirl of stark black uniforms, white bib aprons, and stiff white head-caps. And Madeleine, there at the center: her expression blank, stunned. She holds a glass pitcher half-filled with water in one hand, small wicker basket of guavas hanging from the bend of her other arm. Madeleine dodges the servant with the cheese platter and hurries across the kitchen in the opposite direction, exiting through a door at the back.

The camera returns to the dining table outside, to our feast-in-progress. It narrows its focus again to a shot of Barto, seated as before, wiping his mouth with the linin napkin retrieved from his lap. As the other diners around him continue eating and conversing, Barto folds his napkin and places it on the table beside his plate - empty now except for his knife and fork, positioned at a careful angle to indicate that he has finished eating. He removes a long, kid-leather pouch from a breast pocket, takes out a cigar, returns the pouch to his pocket. Barto stands slowly, the butler putting his bottles down on a crowded sideboard, rushing to pull his chair back. Barto turns, and he walks out of the frame to our left, cigar poised between his fore and middle fingers, as the butler repositions the heavy chair. The camera holds this shot of the table of exuberant, animated diners - in the midst of a toast, their glasses raised - Barto's chair empty at the center.

It transitions to a view of the "behind kitchen" - a separate room, like a pantry - isolated, quiet. With Madeleine standing before the counter, alone. The camera moves from her back as she works at the counter to become a side view: she's peeling guavas for dessert with a short paring knife. The blank expression on her face seems to have hardened - possibly revealing an irritated distraction, frustration, even anger.

The camera, as though it's still unsure of Madeleine's emotions, draws in further for a close-up, not of her face, but of her hands. And the anger in her hands, as she works the sharp knife on a wet guava with her agile fingers, is palpable.

In the background, behind her hands, looming large, is the glass pitcher half-filled with water and soaking guava shells, magnified by the thick, uneven glass: purple-pink, luscious, visceral.

The camera shifts to a shot angled down over Madeleine's shoulder. As she continues peeling the guava with the bright, soaking, visceral-looking shells still visible in the background. On the counter, to one side of the pitcher, is a small mound of discarded guava guts and flayed skin.

Now, from over Madeleine's shoulder, looking down, we see the manicured hand of a white man - his sharp white French cuff with the gold cufflink gleaming at the wrist, sleeve end of his black tuxedo jacket just visible behind the cuff - reaching into the frame from behind Madeleine's back to our left.

Because WE inhabit Madeleine's body now. We can feel the shocking, thrilling, terrifying presence of this man pressing up softly, yet solidly, against our back. We can smell his cologne and cigar after-odor over the pungent guava. And we are no longer sure if the pounding we hear and feel in the hollow of our neck, just below our throat, belongs to him, or to us.

The hand places a cigar down on the wet counter. Then it settles gently over the back of our own hand - stopped, arrested in air, paralyzed - still holding the half-peeled guava.

And as if it suddenly has a mind of its own, as if it can think for itself, our right hand rolls slowly palm-up. The small, wet, gleaming knife balanced there.

Now the white man's other hand reaches around us from the other side. Our right side. This hand taking up the knife, placing it carefully down on the wet counter.

And our left hand – the hand still covered gently by his hand, the hand we cannot even remember or feel still holding the half-peeled guava – our left hand rolls over of its own accord too. Acting on its own, thinking for itself. His hand rolling together with it, inverted now, cupping ours, below. The wet hand above slowly opening, offering, palm-up. Our own two hands. As the half-peeled guava tumbles out and across the counter, and we hear it thud quietly to the floor.

*   *   *

2

Cut to an interior shot of the Archives: Maximos and Homer continue to pile desks
and chairs before the emergency exit door, barricading it from the inside.

Suddenly we hear the explosion of a bazooka - offstage, behind the door -
its blast imploding the metal door with a burst of flame, sending the desks and
chairs flying, knocking Maximos and Homer off their feet.

With the explosion, the school bell rings loudly again, and the bright red
emergency exit sign above the blown-out door is illuminated, blinking slowly.

In the empty doorway we gradually make out two soldiers appearing as the
dust settles. One brandishes his submachine gun, the other his bazooka, while above
them the emergency exit sign continues blinking.

Homer, back on his feet, dust-covered, holds his submachine gun against
his hip. He fires a volley at the soldiers entering, and we watch them slump to
the ground among the tumbled tables and chairs, still clutching bazooka and
submachine gun. The red emergency exit sign above them continues blinking, school
bell ringing, as the dust continues to settle.

Cut to Stoker leading Maximos and Homer out of another, double set of metal
doors at other side of the Archives: the main entrance. We see Homer pull the doors
closed as they exit, the bell subdued.

Cut to a long shot of several soldiers approaching out of the darkness
at the end of a tunnel. They fire their submachine guns at our trio, bullets
ricocheting off the rock walls in little eddies of dust. Homer, in the left
foreground, holds his submachine gun against his hip. He fires a volley at the
soldiers, and we watch them tumble one on top the other to the ground.

Behind Homer, Stoker ducks a bullet that ricochets off a metal pipe with a
loud, reverberating PING. He starts up a ladder through a hatch in the ceiling of
the tunnel. Maximos and Homer follow, the bell further subdued.

The camera shifts to an above-ground shot of a manhole in the middle of
a desolate street, half-melted buildings and debris all around. With a harsh,
scraping noise on the sound track, we watch the heavy manhole cover slowly being
shoved aside from within - and Stoker climbs out, followed by Maximos, and finally
Homer, the school bell finally silenced.

Cut to a panoramic shot of the entrance to Forbidden City, rising ominously
out of the desert to our right. And our trio in the distance - running, carrying
their submachine guns and various equipment - tumbling down the steep sandbank
that descends from the city gates.

Making their escape.

3

The camera fades to an interior shot of the dining room/kitchen in Studio City: Austin and Robin (smartly dressed from work) are seated on stools at the table from Maximos' treehouse, transposed to their home – again suggesting that this scene is part reality, part fantasy, leaning perhaps toward the latter. They are eating takeout Mexican food: burritos wrapped in thin, waxed paper. Scattered on the table before them are several hot-sauce packages and a grease-stained brown paper sack containing tortilla chips. There's a round cardboard container of guacamole, another with rice and beans and a plastic fork; in addition there's a bottle of red wine and two stemmed glasses, half-filled, the small basket with bananas, and the prescription medicine vial.

Austin holds up his peeled-back burrito, chewing.

"What was that all about?"

Robin looks at him skeptically, tortilla chip in hand.

"What was WHAT all about? I'm not in your mind, Austin."

He swallows, smiles.

"Well ... fact is you ARE in my mind – whatever's left of it." He takes a breath. "I was talking about the scene between Barto and Mummy."

"Yeah?" she says guardedly.

"Not sure if it was violent ... or erotic."

Robin is uncertain to what degree she wants be complicit in this.

"Why can't it be both?" she ventures.

Austin considers.

"I see your point," he says.

Robin gestures with her tortilla chip – and a slightly sinking feeling of having stepped over a line, past the point of no return.

"Seems to me it HAD to be both."

He looks at her, unconvinced.

"How's that?"

"Well," she treads cautiously, feels herself miss-stepping despite herself, "If it was ONLY violence, then the only thing it could've led to ... only thing it could've instigated ... was assault."

There's a long pause here.

"You mean ... like physical assault?" Austin swallows. "Rape?"

Her tone is emphatic.

"That's exactly what I mean."

Austin sits up, angry - as if Robin has just insulted him.

"You going to tell me ... I'm the result ... "

He can't bring himself to finish.

"No, Austin. I'm not." She takes a breath. "Two simple reasons: first, your momma loved Barto. You told me so yourself, lots of times. And there's no way love follows that kinda violence. Not if it's legitimate, genuine."

Austin answers after a beat; then backpedals a bit.

"I'm sure Mummy did love him - genuinely, even deeply. At least ... I've always wanted to believe she did."

Robin reaches to take his hand.

"And there's no reason not to, honey. None at all. Just let me finish ... "

"OK," he concedes.

"Second reason is that little knife. Sitting there on the counter, two inches away from her hand."

He looks at her, confused again.

"What about it?" he says.

"Well, way we saw your momma handle that knife on that guava ... wasn't

anybody going to get the better of her. Not till she was good n' ready to give it up.
Not any white man with his pretty fingers ... not with that knife sitting there."

There's a brief silence. Austin's thoughts have already shifted to something
else.

"Why couldn't it just've been a romance? Pure and simple?"

"You mean," Robin smiles. "Like star-crossed lovers?"

"Exactly!" Austin is animated.

"Cause this isn't Hollywood, Austin." She shakes her head. "You know better
than me. It's Port of Spain, Trinidad. 1932. Your momma was a house servant. And Barto
was some kinda wealthy merchant from the upper class. There HAD to be a certain
amount of violence - seems to me - for BOTH of them to break free of their roles."

Austin still looks confused.

"Not their acting roles," she clarifies. "The ones their society locked them
into ..."

"But - "

He hesitates, while Robin completes her own thought.

"... and whatever the social norms were in those days - in Trinidad or
anyplace else - fact is that Barto had his own family ... his wife n' children."

Austin protests again, this time with subdued vigor.

"Still, they had relationship ... some kinda relationship."

Robin pauses, considers.

"Wonder how long they were together?"

"Couldn't've been more than four years."

Robin looks into his face, squeezes his hand.

"Well a lot can happen in four years, baby."

Austin smiles.

"Yeah. Me."

4

Interior shot of the table at StarBucks. Maximos is seated in the center flanked
by Homer (both as humans, without their ape disguises) and Stoker. All wear their
civvies. On the table before them are open scripts and paper cups of coffee.
        Stoker hands Homer his – imaginary – clipboard.

                    STOKER
              Here's the speech
           I wrote for your address
           to the Emergency Assembly.

                   MAXIMOS
              Thank you, Stoker.
             (glances at it briefly)
           Seems . . . fine. How much
               time've we got?

                    STOKER
            (looks at his wristwatch)
              Still a few minutes.

Maximos puts the clipboard aside, distracted.

                   MAXIMOS
                  Good . . .
             (he turns to Stoker)
           There's a personal matter
           I wanted to discuss with you.

                    HOMER
              In that case . . .

He raises the – imaginary – clay jug.

                    HOMER
               Shall I pour?

                   MAXIMOS
           One moment, old-man . . .

                    HOMER
                  (pours)

                    I'll take that
                    as a yes.

                    MAXIMOS
                    (to Stoker)
          ... a rather significant matter.
               It concerns the tape.

                    STOKER
                 (taken aback by
                his thoughtfulness)
               Of course, Maximos.
                  I'm all ears.

                    MAXIMOS
                 How much did
               you actually see?

                    STOKER
          (considers, shakes his head)
               Not a whole lot ...
                 maybe the first
                  few minutes.

                    MAXIMOS
               And what shall we
                 do about that?

                    STOKER
              Nothing, Maximos.
          There's nothing we CAN do.

                    HOMER
                  (drinks)
                Nothing will
             come from nothing ...

                    MAXIMOS
                (ignores him)
               We can go back.

                    STOKER
              And make certain the
             event of another war?
             If we haven't already –
           after ten years of peace?

                    MAXIMOS
            Precisely my point, Stoker.
        The mutants will certainly attack, as
        they did a decade ago. Our returning to
        the Archives won't alter that inevitability.

                    STOKER
            Only accelerate it, Maximos.
            At least now we have time, we can
                prepare our defense.

                    MAXIMOS
                (shakes his head)
        I fear, Stoker, that against contemporary
            warfare - of which the mutants
                are surely capable -
                there IS no defense.

                    STOKER
                    (unsure)
                You mean . . .
            against three H-bombs
                of that capacity?

                    MAXIMOS
                (vehemently)
            I mean against terrorism.
            Against blind faith.
                (slight pause)
            The clash of monotheisms!

                    STOKER
                (even more confused)
                    Religion?

                    MAXIMOS
            To put it rather coarsely, yes.

                    HOMER
                (drains his cup)
            Nonsense . . . science put an
        end to all that voodoo gibberish
                six centuries ago.

                    MAXIMOS
                    (angry)

Old-man, if you don't
lay off the grape juice ...

HOMER
(refills his cup)
Or seven. You gentlemen are
speaking utter nonsense.
Both of you.

MAXIMOS
(angry and exasperated)
Explain yourself, old-man.

HOMER
Well, in the first place, the mutants might
have three H-bombs, but they've got no means of
launching 'em - the shelf-life of the gunpowder
in their booster-rockets expired about as long ago
... as all your voodoo nonsense.
It's about as potent as
baking powder.

MAXIMOS
Meaning?

HOMER
That in order for the mutants to
get their H-bombs from Forbidden City
... all the way here, they'd pretty
much have to FedEx 'em.

STOKER
(after a pause)
And in the second place, Homer?

HOMER
In the second place, there's no reason to
return to Forbidden City to view the
rest of the tape, because -
(smiles mischievously)

STOKER
Because what, Homer?

HOMER
Because I brought it
back with me.

5

Dissolve to an interior shot of Maximos' treehouse; he is seated at the table again flanked by Homer (the two as apes) and Stoker. On the table before them are three calabash cups and the clay jug, as well as Stoker's clipboard. In the kitchen in the background Eva (as chimpanzee) cooks, assisted by Mira.

Stoker looks at his wristwatch.

> STOKER
> It's time, Maximos.

> MAXIMOS
> (still distracted)
> Yes. Thank you, Stoker.
> (to Eva in background)
> Ready, dear?

Our trio stands, Homer quickly filling his cup and taking it up, Stoker his clipboard. Eva and Mira turn from their cooking, and all form a line before the open doorway leading out onto the terrace of the treehouse: Mira first, followed by Eva, then Maximos, Stoker (holding his clipboard), and finally Homer (cup in hand).

> MAXIMOS
> Proceed.

They file ceremoniously out the door.

Cut to a long shot from ground level: the terrace of Maximos' treehouse is in the upper left foreground, slung hammock visible at the rear. Below the terrace are gathered all of the inhabitants of Simian City, including the humans, a low roar emanating from them. They raise up the medallions hanging around their necks as Maximos walks out onto the terrace, some kissing the Hanuman-Obama image. Maximos takes his place at the far edge of the terrace, flanked by Eva and young Mira. A few steps behind them stand Stoker and Homer (occasionally sipping from his cup).

The camera pulls in on Maximos, with Eva and Mira standing at either side. Maximos bends to pat Mira's head affectionately, then turns toward his ape congregation, slowly raising his arms, open-palmed.

The roar is quieted as Maximos lowers his arms, they their medallions.

> MAXIMOS
> My friends, I have called for this
> Emergency Assembly ... because it falls upon

me a most disagreeable duty. Unhappily, I must
inform you of an imminent danger . . .
that now threatens our
ten years of peace.

Again the uproar; Maximos raises his arms to quiet the crowd.

                         MAXIMOS
          In a recent reconnaissance mission to
            Forbidden City, effected by myself,
                 Homer, and Stoker —

             (he turns to acknowledge them,
               Homer raising his cup)

          — we have, unavoidably and most
               unfortunately, re-ignited
                the wrath of that city's
                  mutant inhabitants.

Again the uproar; again Maximos raises his arms to quiet them.

                         MAXIMOS
          We went in peace, in the pursuit of knowledge.
          Yet the mutants responded with such violence . . . as
        to very nearly extinguish our three persons. We survived
        – we made a swift escape – but we did NOT leave the danger
        behind us. Quite the contrary! However, as proud Obomites
         – honoring our pledge and commitment to nonviolence –
              we'll offer the mutants NO offensive. Instead,
               I call upon each of you to stay vigilant.
                Keep a close watch. Prepare yourselves
                 for the unexpected – the unimaginable.
                  Because, my friends, those mutants
                     are crafty. Their methods
                        . . . are devious.

After a pause Maximos bows to the stunned and quieted crowd. He steps back,
as Eva steps over behind Mira, and all line up as before: they file reverentially
back into the treehouse.

6

Cut to the table at StarBucks: Maximos is seated in the middle flanked by Homer (both as humans) and Stoker. All wear their street clothes. On the table are coffee cups and open scripts.

                    STOKER
           That wasn't the speech
           I wrote for you, Maximos.

                    MAXIMOS
           I may have made a few ...
           impromptu emendations.

                    STOKER
           But no defense?
           No preparations at all?

                    MAXIMOS
           None.

                    HOMER
           Nothing will come ...

                    MAXIMOS
           Quiet, old man!

                    STOKER
           We could build a barricade,
           like we did ten years ago.

                    MAXIMOS
           And how effective was that
           barricade against the mutants'
           attack a decade ago?

                    STOKER
           (shakes his head)
           Not effective at all.

                    MAXIMOS
           I fear, that against the methods of
           contemporary warfare, any preparations

we might effect would prove . . .
still more futile.

STOKER
But it feels wrong. To do nothing
but sit around, waiting for them
to launch their attack.

HOMER
(raises his cup)
Might I recommend a pleasant
diversion during the interval?

MAXIMOS
(irritated)
Old-man, faced with a danger as serious
as this, perhaps our best precaution
would be to cut YOU off the
sauce once and –

HOMER
Actually Maximos, I was about
to suggest something else.

MAXIMOS
(exasperated)
Pray tell!
What might THAT be?

HOMER
I was about to suggest
(takes a drink, smiles)
Movie Night.

7

Fade to an interior shot of Maximos' treehouse, early evening. Our trio sit at the
table as in StarBucks (Maximos disguised now as the chimpanzee, Homer as orangutan)
with the clay jug and calabash cups before them. Eva and Mira are busy in the
kitchen, background.

      Homer removes a gray-metal film canister from his backpack sitting on the
floor beside his stool. He holds it up.

                                  HOMER
                              Here it is,
                              gentlemen.

                                STOKER
                         Thing is Homer,
                  that tape's useless to us
                            ... here.

                                  HOMER
                       I beg to sip her.
               (takes a drink, smiles)
                      I mean, differ.

                              MAXIMOS
              Explain yourself, old-man.

                                  HOMER
                 All this religiosity,
                    so little faith.

                              MAXIMOS
               (still exasperated)
           Religiosity's not a word,
              it's not in Webster's.

                                HOMER
                 You get my draft
               ... I mean drift.

                            MAXIMOS
                 I certainly
                 do not.

                            HOMER
                 (gestures over his shoulder)
                      Kindly step over
                    to the window, Maximos.

The camera pulls back as we watch Maximos get up, the annoyed expression imprinted on his face, walk over to the window and look out. Meanwhile, Homer whistles loudly through his fingers.

                            HOMER
                       SHUEEE-WEEET!

He cups his hands around his mouth and calls out to his gorilla "porters" below.

                            HOMER
                    Hoist her up, boys!

Cut to ground level shot from below the treehouse, with Maximos peering out of the window above, still brooding. Below him two gorilla porters stand beside a large and strange-looking machine: Stoker's bicycle disassembled and transformed into a primitive projector - the front wheel repositioned, tires removed from both rims, the pedals turning, in addition to the wheels, a series of crude wooden spools connected by vines, etc. With a large army flashlight positioned to shine into an old hand-mirror, and through the lens of an old Coke bottle.
We see the gorillas begin to hoist the projector/bicycle into the air by a long vine slung over a limb above the treehouse terrace.
Cut back to the interior shot of the treehouse: Homer and Maximos pull the suspended projector/bicycle in through the doorway leading out onto the terrace, and Homer whistles through his fingers again.

                            HOMER
                       SHUEEE-WEEET!

He calls out to the two gorillas below.

                            HOMER
                       That's good.
                    Much obliged, boys.

Homer unties the hoist vine and wheels the projector/bicycle over behind the table, turning it around, setting it up securely on its kickstand.

                    STOKER
                  (suddenly)
              That's my fuckin' bike!

                    HOMER
               Correction, Stoker.
             This WAS your bicycle.
                   (smiles)
                Teach you to lock
               it up in the future.

                   MAXIMOS
                Don't you mean the
                  past, old-man?

                    HOMER
                 Only Stoker's.
           Let's have a look, shall we?
         (grins at them over his shoulder)
              - in the future, they'll
               call this YouTube.

                   MAXIMOS
                  (excited)
             Show us how it works!

     He fits on the reel, fixing the film around the tire rim and behind the Coke
bottle lens.

                    HOMER
              The tape goes on here
              ... and around there.
               And the picture ...

He interrupts himself, turns to Eva and Mira in the kitchen.

                    HOMER
               We're ready, ladies!

     On cue, Eva and Mira come from the kitchen with large gourds of popcorn,
which they set on the table. Then, as Eva lowers grass-woven blinds over the three
windows, Mira unties a vine on the wall to our right, and a canvass screen unfurls
over the open doorway to the terrace - the treehouse going dark. Eva and Mira take
their seats with the others at the table, and Homer climbs onto his projector,
reaching forward to flip on the flashlight.

HOMER
As I was saying . . .

He begins to pedal slowly, and on the sound track we hear the bicycle wheels clicking like an old-fashioned movie projector. Homer reaches down to the bike's crossbar for the water bottle, now filled with red wine, and shoots a stream into his mouth.

HOMER
(smiling delightedly)
. . . the picture
comes out over there.

Homer gestures with his wine-filled water bottle at the screen. The camera follows, focusing on the screen - lighting up a fuzzy white as the picture flickers into view.
Camera pulls in.

III

THE ROMANCE

1

The sequence opens with a long shot of the backyard of the palatial, French Colonial home pictured earlier, as viewed through the screened door of the "behind kitchen". We see, at the far edge of an extensive plot of sparse grass, a low coral-stone wall, with an elaborate and rusted wrought-iron fence running along the top. In the middle of the wall is a fairly wide gap, the two ornate gates backswung. As we look out across the grass, we hear the low clanking roar of an approaching automobile; and suddenly a silver 1930's convertible Cadillac enters the frame to our right, impossibly long, its barrel-hood with the chromed "flying lady" ornament out in front - her hair flowing, breasts protruding - speeding a reckless 35 mph along the dirt alley behind the low coral wall. The car comes to a skidding stop behind the gap in the middle. It stirs up a cloud of dust atop of which the rumbling machine appears to breathe, to float - its tires a soft-looking silvery color with their extra-wide white walls. After another moment, the horn sounds its hoarse, two-noted call.

The camera switches to a reverse shot of the back of the palatial home, as seen from the car. Madeleine hurries out of the screened door, which claps shut loudly behind her. She wears a narrow, calf-length, dark-colored skirt, tight around her belted waist, and a white, sleeveless, snugly-fitting top. Her hair is again arranged in the single braid wound into a crown, with a scarf of Martinican plaid - jade, amber, onyx - tied around it. She carries a picnic hamper hanging from her crook of her arm.

Madeleine is happy, though unsmiling.

The camera shifts to a shot from behind the convertible: we see the back of Barto's head, his slicked-back hair, seated in the driver's seat - as he leans over and throws open the passenger door. We watch Madeleine hurry through the gate, around the car's massive vibrating hood, flanked by stalked headlights looking like crab's eyes. She reaches in and places her picnic basket on the back seat, jumps into the passenger side, pulls the door closed.

We watch from behind as the car pulls away, leaving a cloud of dust hanging in the air before us.

The camera fades to a craned panoramic shot of the convertible Cadillac approaching from the distance, now hurtling a breathless 45 mph along a mountainous coastal road: tropical foliage hugs the sheer rock cliffs to our left, glittering sea stretches away from the shoreline to our right. From our craned position above we observe, as the car approaches, that Madeleine is seated close beside Barto on the front bench seat, her head settled against his shoulder as he drives with one hand on the steering wheel, his other arm around her shoulders, holding her near. The car passes below us as we catch a glimpse of the picnic basket on the back seat, disappearing in a smear out of the frame to our left.

Cut to a shot in through the windshield of the convertible Cadillac, unsteady due to the shuddering car and uneven blacktop, as Barto drives with one hand, Madeline still with her head resting comfortably on his shoulder. In the background behind them we see the bright water to our right, rugged coast to our left, separated by the winding ribbon of pitch.

As he drives, Barto glances over at Madeleine for a moment, then back to the road. Both speak in Trinidadian vernacular, talking loudly over the wind and the roaring engine.

"You know," he says, almost in a shout, "I did want to ask where you get you name from. Write so with a extra 'e'?"

Madeleine raises her head from his shoulder, looking sideways at him.

"Is the French spelling," she says.

Barto shakes his head — he hasn't heard.

"French Spelling," she repeats, louder, her plaid head-tie ruffled by the wind.

"I know that. What I didn't know is you have French blood in you too – besides the Portugee."

"French blood a-tall," she takes a breath. "Mummy name me after some kinda cake. In France they does call it a 'petite madeleine'."

Barto looks at her quickly again – confused, though not because he hasn't heard.

"You mother was a fancy baker?"

Madeleine kisses her teeth – she "stupses" – we watch her lips pucker, but can't hear the exasperated, sucking noise.

"Mummy could bake, but nothing fancy. She read bout that cake in some book." She pauses for a breath. "Mummy call it a 'memory cake', cause the Frenchman telling the story does always eat it to remember things."

"Oh-ho," he says.

"Mummy always say she did want to travel to Paris, only so she could sit in a pastry shop with a proper white cloth and eat that little cake."

Madeleine pauses. "But she never reach Paris."

"Well," he answers directly. "She get you. And you sweet and sof' as any kinda French cake."

Madeleine looks sideways at him, half-smiling.

"You would like to believe so."

One scene melds smoothly into another, this one considerably calmer and quieter: a picnic-in-progress beside a tropical river. Clear sparkling water to the right side of the frame, bamboo-forested riverbank to our left – as the camera slowly draws in on the picnicing couple. On Barto, reclining sumptuously with his head propped against the trunk of a bozé-majo tree (he wears a starched white shirt with the sleeves rolled to mid-forearms, vest, his tie loose at the collar); and Madeleine, lyling beside him on the plaid English picnic blanket – black, red,

taupe – borrowed from her Madam. There's food spread at their feet: a glass bowl
half-filled with pelau, two used plates with utensils and a few leftover raisons
and rice grains, used linen napkins; a bottle of red wine and two half-filled,
cut-crystal tumbler glasses, also borrowed from her Madam. Barto smokes his cigar
comfortably recumbent, Madeleine lying beside him with her arm loosely hugging
his waist, her cheek resting against his chest – eyes closed, dozing.

    The camera draws in still closer on the courting couple, lying together on
the picnic blanket, extending the shot for a moment. Then – with the hand still
holding his lit cigar – Barto reaches and takes up the borrowed, cut-crystal
tumbler glass, half-filled with red wine, and slowly takes a sip.

*   *   *

2

Cut to the subterranean Chapel in Forbidden City: a tea-party-in-progress. The sequence opens with a tight close-up of "Scavenger Bob" (from the bodega scene, wearing his goggles) guzzling brown liquid out of an oversized plastic beer stein, lemon slice sunk to the bottom. While he drinks, over the partying pandemonium, on the sound track we hear the lyrics of Queen's "Bohemian Rhapsody" -

> Is this the real life?
> Is this just fantasy?*
> Caught in a mindwarp ...
> No escape from reality

The camera steps back to a long shot of the underground chapel: security personnel, scavengers, soldiers - mostly male and a few females - all drinking, dancing, partying away. Two mutants are already passed out on the benches. Beneath the altar and bombs sits a boom box, playing at high volume, the stand of arti-ficial candles beside it flickering subtly like a strobe in time to the music. Koch, in his unbuttoned camouflaged army vest, climbs up onto the stone platform beneath the altar supporting the three H-bombs. He's the only mutant who, according to constitution, does not consume alcohol - and is conspicuously sober.
Before he turns around, Koch reaches down to his b-box -

> Momma, 0-0-0
> I don't wanna die ...
> I sometimes wish I'd -

and kills the music. The camera pulls in slightly on Koch as he shouts, interrupting the revelry.

                    KOCH
            O.K. Tea Partiers -
          everybody knock 'em back!

We watch them begin to drain their steins, as Koch gestures with his chin at the two passed-out mutants.

                    KOCH
            Fredrick-fuckin'-H!
            Will somebody douse
            those two goons down.

---

* q: if "just fantasy," is it copyright infringement?
  a: depends on how much money it makes

The camera steps back as we see two of the mutants dump the contents of their steins over the passed out partiers. They shake their heads, liquid flying off their hair as they wake up.

                              KOCH
                    Much obliged, boys.

He removes a small box of matchsticks tucked beneath the cap covering his shiny bald head, then fits on his cap again.

                              KOCH
                        Now listen up.
                  I'm breakin' two a these
                suckers in half. Whoever gets 'em ...

            (we watch him break the matchsticks)

                ... gets to be the two thieves
                    flankin' yours truly.

The camera steps back further as we observe the mutants forming a line before Koch, as if for Communion – a couple of them with their hands folded in prayer, a couple with their arms crossed loosely over their chests. One by one they approach him, kneel, and remove a matchstick from Koch's outstretched hand. The first to draw a short match is "Technician Fred", who had earlier directed the scavenger pillaging the bodega. From the distance we see that he is visibly shocked and shaken. The second to draw a short matchstick is "Scavenger Bob" from the the same scene, still wearing his motorcycle goggles.
     The camera switches to a close-up of Scavenger Bob's face – mortified. He turns as if to bolt, held back by two other mutants, his baseball cap knocked off his head in the fray.
     Behind Scavenger Bob we see Koch approach with a fresh stein of Long Island Iced Tea. He offers it to Bob, who takes the stein, his hand trembling.

                              KOCH
                        Bottoms up!

Scavenger Bob slowly drains the stein, but the panicked expression on his face remains unaltered –

*

* selfie

3

Cut to Maximos' treehouse. All are seated as before in the half-dark, engrossed
in the movie appearing on the screen in the background – the picnic beside the
tropical river. As the scene opens, Maximos rises to his feet, his ape arm raised.

                    MAXIMOS
              Hold up your pedaling
                a second, Homer!

He halts, as the picture freezes behind him –

– and Homer considers his almost empty water bottle.

                     HOMER
               Thank you, Maximos.
               Seems our projector's
               in need of grape juice.

                    MAXIMOS
            More importantly, old-man –
          how appropriate is the content of
              this film for young Mira?

                     HOMER
                    (smiles)
          Does seem a bit racy, doesn't it?

But to answer your question –
I believe it's rated G.P.

MAXIMOS
And what does that mean?

HOMER
Germane for
primates of all ages.

MAXIMOS
Splendid!
(he smiles too)
Then on with the –

Eva cuts him off.

EVA
Unfortunately, dear – even if the content
IS appropriate – it's past Mira's bedtime.
I'll have to ask you boys to continue
your movie tomorrow, so I can
put my daughter to sleep.

MAXIMOS
I beg your pardon, dear.
But Mira happens to be MY daughter too
... and I happen to be King.

He pauses, visibly irritated.

MAXIMOS
And the KING commands his wife and Queen
that HE shall decide his daughter's bedtime
tonight ... and the movie shall continue
– it's just starting to get juicy!

Eva's face reveals her own restrained anger.

EVA
I'd hoped to spare you of this NEWS, Maximos.
But since you're going to pull rank on me
in such a chauvinistic, patriarchal,
and clichéd macho manner –

He interrupts, confused.

                    MAXIMOS
                  Feminism?

                     EVA
          - to put it rather crudely.

She takes a breath, calming herself, and continues.

                     EVA
          ... then I have little choice but to inform
          you that, in fact, Mira MAY be your daughter.
          Or she may NOT. On the other hand, she unquestionably
          belongs to ME ... and her mother commands
              that it is time for her to go to bed.

Close-up of Maximos' face - taken aback. He speaks quietly.

                    MAXIMOS
                Quite right, dear.
          It's best we resume our movie ...
              on another occasion.

4

The camera dissolves slowly into a long, exterior shot of the terrace of Maximos'
treehouse. It's early afternoon, soft luminous sunshine, birds chirping away. We see
the hammock in the distance.
    Slowly we become aware that someone may be lying, hidden, within it.

    The camera draws closer. Now we realize that, in fact, there may be two
individuals hidden from us inside the hammock ... and they seem to be ... slowly
and gently fucking.
    First we hear a few subtle female moans. They gradually speed up, along
with the movement within the hammock ... until we hear HER subdued orgasm.
    The hammock goes still and quiet for a while.
    Then, slowly, the movement within begins again. And we hear a few consider-
ably louder male groans. The movement inside the hammock speeds up – faster and
faster – until we hear HIS not-so-subtle orgasm.

    After a moment, Maximos' head appears above the brim of the hammock,
frazzled and out of breath. A moment later, Eva's head appears (both of them as
chimpanzees). They sit facing one another, as the camera draws in.*

> MAXIMOS
> That was exquisite, my dear.
> (smiles supremely, sublimely)
> The Queen should always come first!

> EVA
> (she smiles too)
> And the King should
> always come second.

    A moment of silence, while we watch Maximos recall the previous evening,
his mood suddenly souring.

> MAXIMOS
> So what did you
> mean yesterday evening
> – Mira might not be my daughter?

Eva pauses; her tone is frank.

———————

* author wiohco to credit the preceding scene with the equivalent one filmed at
Katz's Kosher Deli in WHEN HARRY MET SALLY

                    EVA
        I've always wanted to tell you, Maximos.
        But I knew how difficult it would be for you.
        It was ten years ago ... you were so preoccupied
    preparing your defense against the mutants' attack.
        You hadn't made love to me for days ... Truth is,
            I felt horny. And that afternoon, in the
                outdoor shower stall, I happened
                    to begin ... masturbating.

She pauses, beginning to enjoy the memory, as Maximos' mood sours further.

                    EVA
                I'd only just started up –
                but obviously gotten fairly
                    far along, when –

He cuts her off aggressively.

                    MAXIMOS
                Spare me the details, Eva.

She continues undeterred.

                    EVA
                – when HE happened
            to walk by the shower stall.
                (sighs amorously)
            All dressed up in his uniform,
                and looking so ...

We see what she sees.

                    MAXIMOS
                  So what, Eva?

                      EVA
                     So . . .
                    virile . . .
                     and –

                    MAXIMOS
                And WHAT, Eva?

                      EVA
             – and I invited him in.

                    MAXIMOS
                You invited him IN?

Her voice is earnest.

                      EVA
                      Yes.

                    MAXIMOS
              Into the shower stall?
                or into your . . . ?

                      EVA
                      Both.

Maximos is stunned.

                    MAXIMOS
                    Jesus–H.

                      EVA
           It was ten years ago, Maximos.
       What does it matter? It's old history. Water
    under the bridge. And it's not like you've been entirely
    monogamous over the years – abusing your position of power
     with the First Maidens. All THREE of them! Or need I
       remind you? You'll simply have to swallow some
           of your own medicine. Because the truth is
              you might be Mira's father, or you
               might not. I'm just not sure.

After a protracted, resonant silence, she continues.

                        EVA
              Of course, that was before
              we'd learned anything about ...

                      MAXIMOS
                       About?

Another meaningful pause.

                        EVA
              ... about what he'd done
              to poor Amadeus. I could
                     NEVER ...

                      MAXIMOS
                    (astonished)
                       Gabo?

5

Cut to Studio City, dining room/kitchen: Austin and Robin are seated on stools at the table from Maximos' treehouse, again suggesting the scene's slippery reality. They're eating takeout sushi from plastic containers with chopsticks. On the table before them are several packages of soy sauce and wasabi, a bottle of red wine and two stemmed glasses, half-filled, the basket of bananas and prescription medicine vial.

As Austin swallows a piece of sushi, he turns to Robin.

"You think that scene was pre- or post-?"

Robin looks at him, confused, a piece of sushi suspended between her chopsticks.

"Pre- or post- WHAT, Austin? Don't make me remind you again - I can't read your mind."

"Coital," he says, and swallows.

Robin proceeds cautiously, feeling for a balance between indulging Austin's fantasies, and inflicting pain.

"Maximos and Eva?" she says. "Or Barto and your momma?"

"Barto and Mummy, of course." He pinches up another piece of sushi. "Those monkeys were definitely doin' the nasty - orgasms sounded almost human."

Robin looks at him, speaking gently.

"Austin, they WERE human - actors wearing ape costumes."

"Guess you're right." He smiles at her. "Humans fucking like monkeys."

Robin is drawn in, despite herself. She smiles too.

"Like bonobos."

Now it's Austin's face that shows a momentary confusion.

"A species of apes," she explains. "They fuck like humans."

"Right. That documentary we watched on Prime." He recalls it too. "Those bonobos never let up."

Austin pauses, smiles again.

"Wonder if they have prostates?"

Robin answers without a beat.

"Never held you back, Mr. Stoker."

"Guess I've kept my form up pretty well."

She's pleased to say it.

"You totally have, Austin."

He puts a piece of sushi into his mouth, chewing, shifting the subject.

"What I don't understand – why, all-in-a-sudden, should I become so preoccupied with Barto? His relationship with Mummy? All these concerns about my origins . . . legitimacy . . . why now, at 83-years-of-age?"

Robin considers this a moment.

"Seems to me it's right on time."

Austin raises his brows. "I see your point."

"Good," she says.

"Can't let myself worry too much about worry . . . "

"No, honey, you absolutely can't."

He gives her an indulgent grin. "Next thing you know, I'll lose my mind."

Robin rolls her eyes at him.

"Please don't," she says.

"Probably shouldn't expect myself to understand anyway . . . "

She's not quite sure about this, but nods encouragement regardless.

"Yeah," she says.

Austin completes his thought.

". . . the undeniable reality of one vs thirteen."

Robin tenses her brow.

"Now what do you mean by THAT, Austin?"

"I mean, counting me, Barto had thirteen children. That we know of."

"And?"

"And I've only had the experience of one - my son, Odillo."

Robin looks taken aback, a piece of sushi arrested in the air between her chopsticks.

"Yeah," she says. "Odie . . ."

6

Cut to Maximos' treehouse, nighttime, movie-session-in-progress: Stoker, Maximos and Eva are seated at the table (without Mira), eating popcorn from large gourds. Homer is seated on his projector/bicycle, pedaling slowly, movie showing on the screen in the background.
The camera draws in, revealing –

CARAPICHAIMA, TRINIDAD, 1932; BLACK-AND-WHITE OLD FILM LOOK

*   *   *

The sequence opens with a craned panoramic shot of the convertible Cadillac, approaching from the distance, as if towing a cloud of dust behind it. The car speeds its 45 mph along a dirt road the color of burnt sienna, severing vast sugarcane fields. They stretch away on both sides of the road in wind-blown waves as far as the horizon, purple-jade. In the distance we can almost make out Barto driving, Madeleine sitting close on the bench seat beside him.

The camera shifts again to its unsteady shot in through the convertible's windshield: Barto driving, steering wheel held in one hand, his other arm around Madeleine's shoulders, her head resting comfortably against his shoulder.

In the background we see the receding sugarcane fields, split down the middle by the richly-colored dirt road stretching straight out behind them, the ever-receding cloud of red dust. Madeleine raises her head and turns to look sideways at Barto, again speaking in a near shout over the roar of the car's engine and the wind.

"Is so long I hearing bout this statue from Indra," she says, her Martinican headscarf ruffling.

She explains further.

"Indra does work for Madam Salvatori – she come from South."

"What village we going to?" he asks.

"Carapichaima."

"What again?" he says, like he hasn't heard her properly.

She pronounces it louder, sounding out the syllables.

"Cara-pi-chaima."

"Don't sound East Indian."

"Indra say is Amerindian – Warrahoon or something so."

"Oh-ho," Barto says.

"The temple name Dat-ta-treya."

"Sound Warrahoon too."

"Could be," she says.

Then, with a devious half-smile, "You could ask you wife – she from that part of Venezuela."*

Barto looks chagrined, his eyebrows raised.

"Tell her I ask," Madeleine says.

Now it's Barto's turn to smile. He glances at her briefly, then back at the road.

"She go cut my tail – if she hear bout you." And after a pause, still smiling, "Or shave off half my mustache while I sleeping – she do that once already."

"Good," Madeleine tells him. "Then I could shave off the next half."

Now the camera reverses to a panoramic shot, looking out through the windshield as the car speeds unsteadily along, as seen from the passengers within. Against a cobalt sky filled with bright white clouds, the head and torso of the eighty-three-foot-tall Hanuman statue appears in the far distance – startlingly, magisterially – presiding over the vast, purple-green, wind-blown waves of the sugarcane fields.

---

* the Warrahoons, or War-Warrahoons (from which my grandmother descended), were a tribe of Amerindians native to costal Venezuela, many settling in Trinidad

Now the camera shifts to a craned panoramic shot from behind the convertible, with the gargantuan statue growing still larger, appearing in the closer distance before them over the cane fields.

It shifts again to a shot of the car pulling up before Dattatreya Temple, the base of the Hanuman statue just visible in the frame in the near distance behind the extravagant building. We hear the sound of gravel crunching loudly under the red-stained, white-walled tires.

Cut to a shot of Barto and then Madeleine getting out of the driver's door. Barto shuts it behind her, fitting his arm loosely around her waist. The camera follows them in a tracking shot as they walk together around the tall, smoking front grille of the convertible with the busty totem and her wind-blown hair perched above it, past the entrance to the deserted temple.

They walk toward the base of the statue at the rear of the building.

We watch our courting couple, Barto's arm still hugging Madeleine's waist, both of them leaning back, peering up dizzily through the glare at the statue towering above.

And finally the camera, after its long tease, grants us a full and unencumbered view of the iconic monument.

* * *

Cut to Maximos' treehouse: movie-session-in-progress. Stoker, Maximos and Eva (without Mira) are seated at the table, Homer pedaling his projector/bicycle. All are engrossed in the film appearing on the screen in the background.
Maximos is on his feet, his chimp arm raised, very excited.

MAXIMOS
Hold up, Homer!

Homer stops his pedaling, as the picture of the gigantic statue in the background freezes mid-frame.

He considers his almost empty water bottle.

HOMER
Indeed. Our projector's
pleading for grape juice.

He hands his water bottle to Stoker, who refills it with wine from the clay jug.

MAXIMOS
More significantly, old-man.
I'd like to enquire about
that sacred shrine.

HOMER
(gestures at the screen)
That primitive hoodoo
artifact? What of it?

MAXIMOS
It's extraordinary!
I should like to initiate a
pilgrimage to Cara-pi-chaima immediately.
I should like to proclaim that sanctuary
(he raises his ape arm exultantly again)
- the Mecca of Obamites!

Stoker returns the water bottle, Homer nodding to him as he speaks.

HOMER
You can ask Stoker what became of
his statue - he's Trinidadian.

Austin hesitates, as the image of himself as a youngster flashes through his mind -

*

STOKER
I remember - when I was a boy
of twelve or thirteen - going on a scout
excursion to see that statue. The field-sergeant
tried to climb it, and we had to pull him down
... far as I know, it's still there
in the village.**

---

* Not much of a scout uniform. We had those elastics to hold up our socks - helpful, I
suppose, to keep your legs from getting scratched up by thorns and stung by nettles
on hikes through the forest - also looks like I might have a youthful hard-on!
** another statement which possibly reflects Austin's slippery memory and
unstable mind, since the religious icon was not installed in Carapichima until 2001;
or perhaps a deliberate anachronism on the author's part

Maximos is still standing. He looks from Stoker to Homer again, a puzzled expression on his face.

                    MAXIMOS
                 Explain, Homer.

                    HOMER
             Stoker is quite mistaken.
         (short pause, while he takes a squirt)
            Fact is that seven centuries ago
            the Trinidad government – under Prime
         Minister Manning – gave their statue away
             to the CHINESE, together with their
              uniquely syncretic Trini–soul
                 ... in exchange for a still
                   more MONSTROUS
                      edifice.

                    MAXIMOS
                 (still confused)
                   Politics?

                    HOMER
             To put it rather shrewdly –
            that statue's now a feature of
               Beijing's Disney World.

                    MAXIMOS
              (raises his ape arm again)
                   Blasphemy!

                    HOMER
                  No, bribery:
             it's the highlight of their
               Pirates of the Caribbean.*

* Prime Minister Manning is responsible for commissioning the cyclopean Performing Arts Center (2009) which now dwarfs Port of Spain's once beatific "Savannah" (Queen's Park), located in the heart of the capital: the egregious structure, with considerable public protest (several historic buildings were demolished to accommodate it), was financed by the Chinese and constructed with imported Chinese slave labor.

Cut to interior shot of Austin and Robin's bedroom in Studio City: they are making passionate love. The camera draws in slightly, holds for a moment.

It shifts to a closer shot of Austin and Robin, sitting up in bed, postcoitus. Robin turns toward him, still breathing fast.

"Jesus-H, Austin. That Cialis bout killed me."

He looks at her, also catching his breath.

"What Cialis?"

"Viagra then, baby. Never felt you so big, and hard."

He smiles at her.

"I don't need that junk. That was all me."

"You're kidding."

He nods down at the sheet covering him.

"Nothing medicinal in this body."

"You're right about that - you forgot your memory pills again, Austin ... that's three days running!"

"Might've lost my mind, but I still have my technique."

She smiles as well, despite herself.

"I'll say."

"Got it in my genes, same as Barto."

He pauses, pensive.

"Maximos too," he says. "Come to think of it."

We watch the tranquil expression on Robin's face shift, becoming slightly apprehensive, as she recalls the previous afternoon. Her tone is serious.

"Austin, honey ... "

He looks at her.

She's cautious yet determined.

"There's somethin' ... remember how you were saying bout Odie being your only?"

He smiles again, mischievously.

"Don't tell me you're pregnant? Postmenopausal?"

Now her expression betrays a rising frustration.

"This is serious, honey. And the truth is ... I've been thinking about it – living with it – for a long time."

He turns to her, his expression equally serious.

"Sounds like you need to get something off your chest."

"I do, Austin. And I realize it's absolutely the wrong time – considering you're going through your 'legitimacy' crisis and all – but honey, when IS the right time to say something difficult? Something that's been weighing on you for years?"

There's a poignant silence here, which Austin finally interrupts.

"Not sure how to answer that one ... but sounds like this is something I really don't want to hear."

"No, I'm sure it isn't." Robin's look is sympathetic, yet resolute. "Well, remember when it was we first got together?"

Austin sits up, animated. "1973. We'd just come off the set. I met you in StarBucks."

She looks at him, frustrated again.

"Wasn't any StarBucks in 1973, Austin."

"Whatever the coffee shop was called."

"Forget the coffee shop. What FILM were you making, Austin – in March, 1973 – when we first met, and eight weeks later I was already pregnant with Odie?"

"I was working on . . . ASSAULT, I think."

"And who was I dating before I met you? When we first started going out . . . and you were making ASSAULT?"

She pauses, clarifies, "The SIMIAN one?"

"I don't . . . "

"He introduced us, Austin. Said he'd been trying to get us together for the longest time. And then he finally did . . . "

She waits a beat before adding, "In the coffee shop."

Austin pauses also, his expression a combination of disbelief and unwelcomed revelation, his voice restrained.

"Gabo?"

9

Cut to a panoramic shot of Simian City: it's late afternoon, resplendent sunshine. We see, as in our initial picture of the ape civilization, the industrious community – ape farmers work the fields, female apes prepare food, etc. As we watch, we gradually make out on the sound track the low grinding hum of a distant motor vehicle. Then, over the hum, we hear subdued rock music – an occasional muted shout.

Cut to a panoramic shot of the desert outside Simian City: the school bus from the mutants' garrison approaches from a distance, its red lights blinking, speeding along and sliding in the desert sand. Rock music blasts through a loudspeaker mounted on top the bus – Queen's "We are the Champions." The mutants in the bus are all partying, shouting, several hanging out of the windows with their steins sloshing Long Island Iced Tea. The driver, Scavenger Bob (wearing his motorcycle goggles), reaches his arm out of the window, vigorously ringing his school bell.

Return to the previous, pacific shot of Simian City – with the sounds of the approaching school bus, the music and partying mutants, growing louder.
Slowly, in the distance, we watch the bus enter the frame in the upper right background. Now we see that it is towing a flatbed trailer, containing several tall objects covered over with a thick gray tarpaulin. We continue watching the bus in the distance, pulling its trailer through the dirt and dust, mutants partying and shouting, playing the loud music – as the bus slowly begins to circle Simian City. In the distance we also see some of the apes pause from their work, shading their brows, staring away at the bus and pointing at it, uncomprehending.
Cut to a long shot of the bus driving up the main street of Simian City – the apes staring mystified as it speeds past – a handful of young chimps and black human children now running behind, throwing stones at it. They come to a halt beneath Maximos' terrace as they watch the bus speed on ahead, departing Simian City.

Cut to a panoramic shot from behind the bus – speeding through the desert just beyond Simian City. It comes to a screeching halt, raising a cloud of dust. We watch the stop sign extend as the doors swing open with a rusty squeal, and Koch exits and steps down – surely the only sober mutant aboard the bus. The expression on his face is all business. Koch walks around to the back of the bus and unhitches the flatbed trailer, covered with its dusty tarpaulin. From the distance we watch him whistle through his fingers –

                    KOCH
               SHUEEE-WEEET!

- his whistle subdued by the distance and the loud rock music. Koch waves his hand above his head.

The driver hears the signal, the stop sign folds in and the bus of partying mutants takes off again, leaving Koch and the flatbed trailer behind. It speeds away, sliding in the desert sand – dust trailing behind, music fading on the sound track.

10

Cut to close-up of Maximos and Eva, sitting in their hammock on the treehouse
terrace, positioned as before, postcoitus. Maximus turns to Eva, his expression
revealing his irritation.

                    MAXIMOS
             ... didn't even think it
             was genetically possible.

                    EVA
                   What?

                    MAXIMOS
             Or physiologically.
               (he pauses)
             For a chimpanzee to ...
             MATE with a gorilla.

                    EVA
                 (remembers)
             Oh, it's possible alright.

                    MAXIMOS
               (more disgruntled)
             I'd rather not know.
               (he pauses again)
             Truth is, I'm
             jealous.

     Eva's expression and her tone shift from a distracted recollection, to
something much more serious.

                    EVA
             Gabo's DEAD, Maximos.
             YOU killed him. How can you
             be jealous of someone who's dead?
             Of something you're not even sure of?

                    MAXIMOS
             It's not simply that he throws into
             question my role in Mira's procreation.
             He undermines my manhood.

My position as –
(he pauses)
Primary Procreator.

She responds with a look of profound exasperation.

EVA
Jesus–H.

MAXIMOS
And the sacred
institution of marriage ...

Now she's blatantly angry.

EVA
Please!

MAXIMOS
If he was just another chimp.
Truth is, I feel ...
diminished.

EVA
What difference does it make?
We're all the same species.

MAXIMOS
Same species ...
but gorillas are
(pauses)
inferior.

EVA
Not in the hammock,
I assure you!

MAXIMOS
It's scientific fact, Eva. Whether
you want to admit it or not. They're
less intelligent, their skins are
darker, they're more ...

                         EVA
                 More what, Maximos?

                       MAXIMOS
                    More monkey.

The camera returns to the former panoramic shot from behind the old school bus, as it speeds away through the desert beyond Simian City. Inside, the mutants party away, music blasting. The bus screeches to a halt with its rusty brakes, stirring up a cloud of dust, as we watch the stop sign fold out and the doors swing open with a squeal – and Technician Fred from the bodega scene is violently shoved out, tumbling to the sand, his stein spilling.

The stop sign is withdrawn and the bus speeds away, leaving him behind. The camera holds this shot for a few seconds – the bus speeding through the desert, sliding in the sand, music blasting.

It screeches to a halt for a second time, a cloud of dust rolling over the bus. The stop sign extends as the doors swing open again, and Scavenger Bob from the same scene is forcibly kicked out by several mutants. He struggles desperately with them, but still manages to hang onto his school bell. He also tumbles to the sand as the stop sign folds in, and the bus of partying mutants speeds away through the desert.

12

Cut to a medium shot of Austin and Robin sitting up in bed, positioned as before, postcoitus. Austin's former startled expression now betrays an undisguised irritation.

"But Gabo was white. I'd always assumed Odillo got his fair skin from me ... from Barto."

An image of himself as a youngster flashes through Austin's mind.*

Robin looks at him.

"I'm pretty positive he did, Austin. I'm just trying to be truthful with you, after holding it in for so long."

She pauses.

"I'm trying to be truthful with myself."

"Sure," he says. "But if I'm going to be truthful ... it makes me angry. Makes me feel fuckin' resentful. And the fact that Gabo's a white man only makes it worse."

Robin considers this.

"It's interesting. You seem, somehow, to venerate Barto's whiteness ... yet you resent Gabo's."

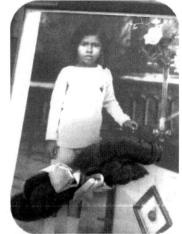

---

* As a child I also had pretty hair, with lots of curls, just like Mummy. And in those days it was the style to grow it out long, for boys too – if they had good hair. Show it off, I suppose. Mummy used to comb it out with coconut oil. I remember on the day before my fourth birthday – just before I started school – Mummy put me to stand on a chair on the front gallery, and she cut off all my locks. She tied one of those locks with a blue ribbon and kept it for me – if I didn't tell you, you'd think it was a turd!

He answers directly.

"That's not how I see it!"

"You're right. Maybe you don't see it."

She pauses, then continues.

"But whatever color skin he had, my relationship with Gabo existed before I even met you. And if it wasn't for Gabo . . . we probably never would've met in the first place."

Austin's anger remains.

"Thing is, I can't imagine NOT being Odillo's father."

She considers this well.

"You could do the gene test? You n' Odie? If you need to know for sure."

He looks away, fearful.

"But what if . . . " he swallows. "What if Odillo DIDN'T get my genes? Or I didn't get Barto's genes?"

"Well, that's just a chance you'll have to take, Austin. If you need to know the answer for sure."

She pauses, then continues.

"And the truth – independent of anybody's genes – is that what Odie got from you is devotion. Years of it. Dedicated love and care."

She pauses again, for emphasis.

" . . . if you ask me, THAT'S the true meaning of fatherhood."

Austin reflects on this a moment.

"What I didn't get from Barto, I suppose."

"No, you didn't." She turns to him. "So give yourself a break."

He's not listening, caught up in his own thoughts.

"Maybe . . . it was what Barto COULDN'T give me? What his society n' social standing and all wouldn't ALLOW him give me? That's another thing I've always wanted to believe ... "

He pauses, sounding defeated.

"We'll never know!"

Inappropriately – and totally out of context, out of character – Robin smiles at this.

"We might," she says, "find out."

Austin is nonplussed.

"How ... for Christ's sake?"

She smiles still.

"Your MOVIE, Austin."

*   *   *

13

The sequence opens with a panoramic shot of the convertible Cadillac in the distance, again speeding along the burnt sienna road severing vast, purple-jade, wave-blown sugarcane fields. Again towing its rust-colored cloud of dust. The camera switches to a craned shot from behind the speeding car. We see Barto driving, Madeleine sitting close, as the car slows and turns onto another dirt crossroad, leaving the cane fields behind. After a moment the car slows once more, passing though a rusted wrought-iron gate arching above the road, "Chaguaramas" inscribed over the arch.

The camera shifts to a shot of the car pulling up to a small estate house, halting before it. Over the sound of the rumbling motor we hear the horn bellow its two-throated donkey call. We look in through the car's windshield for a close-up of Barto and Madeleine, as Barto reaches for the ignition key to stop and silence the engine.

He turns to Madeline, looking into her eyes, kissing her passionately.

The camera shifts to a medium shot of Barto and Madeleine, getting out of the driver's door. He shuts it behind her just as Junior, the East Indian overseer of the estate, approaches. He is short in stature, older, barefoot and dustily barelegged. Junior wears a dhoti and "merino" undershirt, Hanuman medallion on a gold chain around his bony neck – faint white smudge of a Hindu tilak marking his brow.

The overseer reaches energetically to shake Barto's hand, though his brown face registers no discernable emotion. Behind them Madeleine reaches into the back seat of the convertible to retrieve the picnic basket.

Barto puts his arm affectionately around his overseer's shoulders. He gently turns the smaller man, steering him toward the house as they talk. The two walking together slowly, Madeleine at Barto's other side.

He looks down warmly at his overseer.

"June-ya, boy, is tree weeks I ain't see you, nuh. So much of work in town! What happening on the estate?"

"We baggin' tonka tomorrow, boss. I could give you five-six sack to carry back."

"Is good I come then."

When they get to the door Barto takes his arm from around his overseer's shoulders, and Madeleine hands Junior the picnic basket. The overseer reaches with his free hand to turn the knob and pull the door open. He takes a step back, bowing formally first for Madeleine to enter, then Barto.

Junior straightens and shuts the door behind them. He turns and walks off with the picnic basket.

The camera holds this shot of the small estate house for a moment.

It dissolves to an interior view of the bedroom within. The camera pauses for a moment, while we internalize what we're seeing, slowly drawing in on Madeleine's naked back: her long hair cascading in waves over her confidently-held, elegant, burnt-sienna shoulders.

She is perched above Barto on the bed, as they make passionate love.

The camera holds this shot for a second.

IV

THE WAR

*   *   *

The sequence opens with the familiar, panoramic shot of Simian City. It's late afternoon, workers still in the fields, women preparing food, etc. We gradually make out the distant shouts and laughter of several children, but then we hear other, more discordant sounds that jar uncannily with the usual pacific atmosphere of this scene: the muted noise of metal scraping against hard ground, muffled cursing, occasional crack of a whip.

In the distance, one by one, three white men enter the frame in the upper right background, naked except for white loin cloths and red baseball caps (we can't make their faces out yet). Each carries a bomb on his back by utilizing the overgrown scapulars as a kind of harness – their heads and necks fitted though the chain loops, in such a manner that the photograph portraits hang over their bare chests, their arms reaching behind them to clutch at the bombs' side fins. They half-carry, half-drag their bombs along the dirt road, several young apes and black children following, taunting them.

From far away we watch one of the white men suddenly stumble forward under his bomb; he is crushed brutally beneath it. Laughing, the handful of young apes and black kids run ahead to help lift the bomb erect, assisting the man back onto his feet in his scapular-harness. And the slow procession starts off again.

Cut to a medium shot of Koch dragging "Drumpf II" on his back, Technician Fred dragging "Drumpf I" and Scavenger Bob, "Jr".

All three are scarred, bleeding from various wounds. As they lug their bombs along the dirt road, the kids follow, throwing stones at the trio, jeering at them. A young orangutan will occasionally run up and beat one of them with a thorny branch; an older black girl has a whip with which she occasionally strikes one of the trio.

Cut to a long shot along Main Street as the trio approaches, dragging their bombs, followed by the chimps and children, and now also a handful of adult apes and black humans. They eventually come to a halt beneath the terrace of Maximos' treehouse.

Exhausted, the trio set their bombs erect on the ground behind them, while Maximos – his afternoon nap interrupted by the commotion – walks to the edge of the terrace above, wearing his nightrobe.

MAXIMOS
(yawns)
Who dares inter-
rupt my royal nap?
(looks below, considers)
And what is this hideous,
most vulgar display?

Koch, reeling with exhaustion, ducks out from inside his scapular.

                    KOCH
          Thought we'd pay you a lil'
          visit, Maximos. Sorry our
          timing's not convenient.

From his perch on the deck it seems that Maximos notices only the three
diapered white men, and not the gray-metal bombs half-hidden behind them.

                  MAXIMOS
          What's inconvenient
          is your state of dress
          - or shall we say un-dress.
          (he studies the trio)
          Furthermore, your hygiene is
          deplorable. All three of you. Kindly
          clean yourselves up, and come
          back after my nap.
          (turns toward his hammock again)
          And put on some fresh diapers!

The camera draws in on Koch in the center of the frame, with the inhabitants of Simian City gathered in the right background - gesturing, muttering,
clearly confused. Koch removes the small box of matchsticks tucked beneath the cap
covering his shiny head.

                    KOCH
          Sorry, Maximos. But that
          just ain't going to
          be possible.

He turns around and reaches down toward the long fuse curling up from
the base of "Drumpf II". Koch strikes a match, cupping it with his palms - we see
the match flare, then a bright sparkle at the end of the fuse - as a puff of smoke
rises and cries of alarm erupt from the apes in the background.

Homer appears, strolling up casually to Koch, calling out to Maximos above.

                   HOMER
          Before you get too deep
          into your nap, Maximos ...
          just thought I'd point out
          a little something.
          (he halts beside Koch)
          In case you happen to

stumble across one again
in the future.

By this point Maximos, standing on his terrace above, has turned around. He looks down at Homer and Koch below.

                    MAXIMOS
              And what might that
                be, old-man?

Homer draws the ape finger with his Harvard school ring across his throat.

                    HOMER
            Undoubtedly your past:
            (he pauses dramatically)
          done-for, belly-up, ka-put.

                    MAXIMOS
                (exasperated)
          Explain yourself, old-man.
          And kindly do so in language
          that even Maximos can understand!

Homer puts his arm around Koch's shoulders to hold him up.

                    HOMER
              This gentleman is what
            you call a suicide bomber.
            (he pauses, reflecting)
          Comes from a long line, stretching
          right back to good ol' J.C. Himself.
              Back in the year ONE.
                Only HIS bomb was
                 metaphorical.

Maximos is further exasperated. He shakes his his head – a knotted expression on his chimp face.

                    MAXIMOS
          No other way to put it, Homer.
          But what you're saying sounds to
            me like utter bullshit.

                    HOMER
              (smiles broadly)
              If the diaper fits ...

By this point all of the inhabitants of Simian City have gathered in background behind the trio. Now in loud uproar, they point anxiously at the sparkling fuse, as it grows threateningly shorter. Also, by this point, Technician Fred and Scavenger Bob have ducked from out of their scapulars as well.

Homer calmly shoots a long stream of wine from his bota, extinguishing the sparkling fuse - we see the sparkle go out, a small puff of smoke rising.

He looks up at Maximos again.

                         HOMER
             Now that our little emergency
           has been successfully averted, you can
                return to your nap, Maximos.

He turns and speaks to the group of young apes and kids who'd previously taunted the trio, gathered just behind him.

                         HOMER
             And I'll ask you boys to kindly
               escort these three gentlemen
                 ... OUT of Simian City.

The crowd of apes parts to make way for Koch, Technician Fred and Scavenger Bob as they begin stumbling - with as much haste as they can summon - along Main Street of Simian City, leaving their bombs behind.

As directed by Homer, the young apes and kids throw stones at them, etc., urging them on their way.

2

Cut to Austin and Robin's dining room in Studio City: they are seated on stools at the table from Maximos' treehouse, eating sushi from plastic trays with chopsticks. On the table are multiple packages of soy sauce, wasabi, the bottle of red wine and two half-filled stemmed glasses, in addition to the prescription medicine vial (no bananas).

Austin is distracted, pensive.

"Here's the thing: Barto's relationship with Mummy – to the extent that it was genuine – was doomed on so many levels."

He pauses.

"Yet somehow they found a way ... I appreciate that."

She offers encouragement, support.

"You have to, Austin. You're the result." She takes a breath, "The blessing."

He continues.

"In some regards, I even admire their relationship."

"It wasn't easy. Love isn't easy ... no matter what Hollywood likes to say."

"I've always had this ... image in my mind, ever since I was a kid – maybe it was a dream?"

"Yeah," she nods, offers encouragement again.

Austin is caught up in his reverie.

"They're both floating in the clouds. And mummy's reaching up – I see her clear as day – with Barto more nebulous, more a kind of formidable presence, looming above her ... He's all foggy except his hand, that same white man's hand I recognize somehow, reaching down to her."

Robin looks at him, suspicion creeping in.

"Yeah," she repeats, a bit slower.

Austin is rapt, consumed by his musing.

"They held on . . . they found a way to hold on."

There's mild skepticism in Robin's tone.

"Easier to reach down, honey . . . than it is to reach up."

Austin's still absorbed.

"But the hand reaching down holds all the weight!"

Robin finally shakes her head.

"Only in the metaphor, Austin . . . not in real life." She pauses. "And seems to me your momma had her feet planted pretty solid. She didn't need a man, even Barto, to hold her up."

Austin's look reveals an undisguised deflation, irritation.

"You got to admit it's a pretty compelling image, though . . . metaphor, or whatever you want to call it."

"It's misleading, Austin."

He looks at her, clearly defeated.

"I suppose."

Robin tries to be encouraging, despite knowing better.

"We'll see, baby."

She smiles, continues.

"Who knows? Maybe Barto'll prove me wrong."

3

Cut to Maximos' treehouse, movie-session-in-progress. Maximos, Eva and Stoker are
seated at the table eating popcorn, Homer riding his projector/bicycle.

 The camera draws into the screen: it opens with a shot looking out through
the screened door of the "behind kitchen", across the backyard of the Colonial home.
It's early evening, the air completely still, silent - not even the birds chirp. The
convertible Cadillac, with its white-walled tires, is parked on the other side of
open gate, engine off. The camera holds this shot for a long half-minute.
 It shifts to a reverse shot of the back of the Colonial home, as seen from
the car. The camera holds another half-minute. Eventually, Madeleine steps out,
screen door clapping shut loudly behind her. She's shockingly pregnant. Uncom-
fortably dressed in the black, snugly-fitting servant's uniform, the starched
white bib-apron is tied awkwardly around her hugely swollen abdomen and
enlarged breasts.

 The camera follows in a tracking shot as she lumbers across the yard,
shifting to a view of her back as she walks with difficulty toward the car. We
continue to watch Madeleine's back as she stands beside Barto, eclipsing our view of
him.
 The camera holds this shot for another long half-minute, as clearly words
pass between them, their tone and tenor unclear. After a time we hear the engine
start with a grinding noise - startling us, as it's the first harsh sound, other
than the screen door clapping shut, since the sequence began. Then the car pulls
away, with the sound of gravel crunching loudly under its soft-looking tires.
 The car disappears out of the frame to our left.
 The camera holds this shot of Madeleine's back as she stands in the middle
of the open gateway, elaborate and rusted wrought-iron gates backswung at either
side; Madeline unmoving, staring off into the vacant, silent distance - another
half-minute.

4

Close-up of Austin, pushing in the door of the portable toilet beside the Simian City set, "Johnny-on-the-Spot" stenciled on it in black spray paint.

The door opens into the Men's Room at StarBucks, as Austin rushes in. We watch his back as he stands before the urinal, pulls down the waist of his track pants with his legs spread, peeing. The camera draws in for a close-up side-view of Austin's face, his cheeks puffed as he tolerates the pain, becoming the familiar, beatific expression. We watch as he shakes out the last drops.

Cut to a medium shot of Austin, pulling in the Men's Room door, "M" inscribed on the other side.

The camera follows as he walks past a few tables with seated patrons, script folded under his arm. As he continues, it appears that Luke Skywalker is seated at one of the more distant, less visible tables in the background behind Austin, drinking coffee with Princess Leia - both still in costume and fresh off the set.

As the camera follows Austin, for an instant we see that in the unclear distance, seated at the far side of the table between Luke and the Princess, facing the camera, is Yoda, his ears broadly protruding.

Cut to Austin taking his seat at the table between Maximos and Homer (both as humans, dressed in their civvies), paper coffee cups and open scripts before them.

Homer looks up from his script.

                    HOMER
          That urination took you
          light-years, Austin!

                    AUSTIN
          It felt galactic.

The attendant from the earlier scene arrives suddenly, holding a large paper cup of coffee; he puts it down on the table before Austin.

                    ATTENDANT
          Grande neegro,
          two EX shots.

He departs, same conceited look on his face. Homer shakes his head indignantly at him.

                    HOMER
          What's that jerk's problem?

(he turns back to his script)

                    ...think it's your
                    line, Maximos.

                         MAXIMOS
                         Yes...

Maximos reads silently. After a moment he contorts his face, assuming a
deeply distressed expression.

                         MAXIMOS
                    It's a nightmare!
                    Like sleeping on top
                    of three live bombs.

                         HOMER
                    You talking about the
                    First Maidens again? Or your
                    domestic situation?

Maximos' expression is now exasperated as well as distressed.

                         MAXIMOS
                    Kindly appreciate my
                    frustration, Homer. I feel
                    like I'm sitting around waiting
                    to be blown sky-high!

                         HOMER
                    ...another matter to take
                    up with your wife, I believe.
                    Or those three nubile –

Austin cuts him off, his tone contrastingly serious.

                         AUSTIN
                    What about dismantling
                    the bombs, Homer?

Cut to a reverse shot of Homer: in the unclear distance, among the patrons
seated at the other tables, we seem to make out Chewbacca and Han Solo, also fresh
off the set – but we only see them for a flash.
Homer peers into his cup, contemplating.

                    HOMER
              Guess I could . . .
                give it a shot.

Switch to a reverse shot of our trio seated at the table.

                    MAXIMOS
          But isn't that an extremely delicate
          operation? requiring extraordinary
            concentration and precision?
              (shakes his head, doubtful)
                one false move and . . .

The camera reverses to the shot of Homer. Seated at the table in the
background we see that the patrons are, indeed, Chewbacca and Han Solo (Harrison
Ford). And sitting at the far side of the table between them, wearing a bright red-
and-white kitschy Hawaiian shirt, is the celebrated mythologist and screen writer,
Joseph Campbell.

                    HOMER
                  (smiles)
                Doomsday.

The camera widens its view of our trio, with the other trio (Chewbacca, Solo,
Campbell) seated at the table behind them - all drinking their coffee and chatting
away animatedly. Maximos turns to Homer.

                    MAXIMOS
              Then our first task
            shall be to sober you up!

                    AUSTIN
            Don't be so sure, Maximos.

                    MAXIMOS
                  Meaning?

                    AUSTIN
            Ever see Homer first
            thing in the morning?

                    MAXIMOS
              Not by choice,
              I assure you.

                    AUSTIN
              Shakes like a leaf.

                   MAXIMOS
                   (crossly)
                 You mean to
                 tell me ...

                    AUSTIN
             That in order for Homer
           to dissemble those bombs ...

Close-up of Homer, smiling, cup raised in a toast.

                    HOMER
              We'll have to keep
             our SAPPER in ample
            supply of grape juice.

       Behind him Chewbacca, Solo and Campbell raise their coffee cups and touch
them together.

5

Interior shot of Maximos' treehouse: he's seated at the table flanked by Homer (both as apes) and Stoker, with the clay jug and calabash cups before them. When the scene opens Maximos' cup is already raised.

                    MAXIMOS
              Never thought I'd say it,
              Homer. But nothing makes me
              happier than raising this
              calabash to your success.
              (gestures with his cup)
              Well done, old-man!

Homer and Stoker raise their cups also, clinking them against Maximos.

                    HOMER
              Oh ye of little spirits!

                    STOKER
              You truly are a poet
              and a sapper.

                    MAXIMOS
              ...and now that your gorilla
              porters've dumped those defunct
              bomb canisters over the cliff,
              we can put this distasteful
              little episode behind us
              once and for all.

                    HOMER
              (after a pause)
              Not so fast, Maximos.

Maximos looks at him, his chimp face slightly contorted, confounded again.

                    HOMER
              Fact is, we've
              still got a city full
              of angry mutants out there
              - and they're not too neighborly.

                    MAXIMOS
              Nothing much we can
            do about that, I'm afraid.

                     HOMER
          You're quite right to be afraid,
          Maximos. Cause old Vesuvius insisted on
        dumping your entire armory over the cliff,
         along with those bombs - said he's been
            wanting to do it for centuries.

Maximos raises up his medallion, indignantly.

                    MAXIMOS
              Without MY consent?!

                     HOMER
           Somebody's got to take a stand on
         the weapons laws - if our government's
           going to behave like a buncha -

                    MAXIMOS
                 (cuts him off)
            Then we no longer have a
           SINGLE weapon of defense!?

                     HOMER
           None. Furthermore, your Military
          General has retired to the Caymans.

                    MAXIMOS
                (deflated again,
                openly fretful)
                 We're doomed!

                     HOMER
            I'd beg to disharmonize -
         or shall we say, proselytize.

                    STOKER
                (after a pause,
                his tone serious)
             You mean - convert the
           mutants to OUR pacifistic
           and tolerant beliefs?

                    HOMER
            In a manner of preaching.

                    MAXIMOS
            And how do you propose to
            accomplish THAT, old-man?

                    HOMER
            (he hesitates, considering)
            How do you imagine, Maximos?
            What makes the heart soar?

Homer smiles, raises his ape eyebrows.

                    HOMER
            - I'll give them poetry.

He takes up the clay jug, turning and examining it closely.

                    HOMER
            "Break a vase, and the love
            that reassembles the fragments
            ...is stronger than that love
            which took its symmetry for
            granted when it was whole." *

    There's an uncomfortable moment, while Maximos' face reveals his
embarrassment at Homer's deeply expressed sentiments.

                    MAXIMOS
            This is nothing, numbskull!

                    HOMER
            As a perfect fool
            would say!

He takes a sip, raises his cup.

                    HOMER
            ...worst case scenario
            I've got my other ministry.

————————

* Homer here quotes the St. Lucian poet Derek Walcott from his Nobel Prize Lecture
(or Walcott quotes Homer?)

                    STOKER
                (thoughtfully)
          But you can't go back to
        Forbidden City alone, Homer.
              It's too dangerous.

Maximos chimes in after a pause, somewhat regretfully.

                    MAXIMOS
                Stoker's right.
            Whatever you mean to
        attempt out there in that hellhole,
          we'll have to accompany you.

                    HOMER
               (shakes his head)
         You goons'll just get in my way.
          Besides, Stoker's still got ...
             (he interrupts himself)
          - Anybody ever teach you to
            ride a bike, Maximos?

                    MAXIMOS
          An undignified pastime,
        I've done it once or twice.

                    STOKER
                 What for?

                    HOMER
               So my absence
        (drinks, raises his cup again)
          - won't curtail your movie.

6

LAVENTILLE, TRINIDAD 1934; BLACK-AND-WHITE OLD FILM LOOK

The sequence opens with a shot of the yard behind a BARRACKS HOUSE, as seen through the back screened door: weeds and patches of reddish-brown dirt, an outhouse to one corner, small outdoor kitchen to the other. Along the back periphery of the yard runs a rusted wire fence, with an open gateway in the center.

The convertible Cadillac enters the frame in the right background, behind the fence, driving slowly along the dirt alley, maneuvering potholes. The car comes to a stop behind the open gate, and after a second the horn sounds.

Cut to a reverse shot of the back of the two-story barracks house, as seen from the car: clean, orderly, but showing privation – the camera holding this shot for a second.

The screened door opens and Madeleine steps out, door clapping shut behind her. She's barefoot, wearing an old, faded dress, her long hair down around her shoulders – comfortably confident in her beauty and in her motherhood. She carries two-year-old Austin on her hip, moving briskly. We see that she is smiling fully for the first time.

The camera follows Madeleine as she walks toward the car, shifting to a view of her back as she carries young Austin. Holding this shot for a second of Madeleine standing beside the car, eclipsing Barto, Austin held against her hip.

Switching to a shot from behind the car, angled slightly down from above. Barto has the two-year-old standing on his lap as he sits in the driver's seat, Austin's little hands holding the steering wheel – while Barto talks to Madeleine. After a few seconds he hands Austin back to her, and she settles him on her hip again. Barto hands over a folded clump of bills, which she tucks into her brassiere. He starts the car and drives off, as Madeleine turns and starts toward the house.

Cut to a shot viewed from the backyard gate: we see Madeleine from behind, walking briskly toward the house with Austin held against her hip, entering the screened door; it clapping shut.

Hold this shot of the barracks house and yard for a second.

*

* flower pot a "birthing gift" from Madam Salvatori

7

Austin and Robin's Studio City dining room: they are seated on the crudely-
fashioned stools at the table from Maximos' treehouse, bottle of red wine and two
half-filled stemmed glasses before them, along with the plastic prescription
medicine vial (no food).

Austin speaks first.

"That's the house I grew up in."

Robin looks at him, unsure of his meaning, her tone cautious.

"Which house is that, honey?"

He explains.

"Barracks house in Laventille. House I grew up in."

"Oh," she pauses. "Then how come you didn't show it to me when we went to
Trinidad?"

He answers her straight.

"I couldn't have."

"Too emotional?"

Austin answers her directly again.

"Not at all."

Now Robin's face registers a disturbed concern.

"Because," she takes a breath, swallows. "The house only exists in your
imagination?"

Austin screws his face up at her, like she's bonkers.

"That house was demolished before you were born."

"Oh," she says.

"Now it's a KFC."

"Huh." She sounds relieved.

Austin's face shows that he's drifting back, reminiscing his childhood.

"Amazing. All I remember of that house is how happy we were, Mummy and me. With Uncle Bert and Auntie Emily and my three cousins – Rod, Ruthie and Benny – living upstairs."

She's not sure how to answer. How can she be responsibly emboldening for him?

"Seems like a happy way to grow up, baby."

Austin is mind-traveling.

"Looking at that house . . . you'd think we were poor. But the truth is, I can't remember wanting for anything. Somehow mummy always found a way to make sure we had all we needed – to give us a decent, comfortable, middle-class life – all I needed, anyway."

"She did it alone?"

"Uncle Bert helped. And Barto must've given her money. First few years."

"Madeleine never had another man?"

He answers definitively.

"No."

"You think?"

His tone is resolute.

"I would have known. Uncle Bert and Auntie Emily would have known."

Robin finally feels herself pulled in, surrendering.

"Madeleine was totally dedicated – she was in love!"

It's Austin who pauses now, hesitates.

"With Barto?" he asks. "Or with me?"

There's another short silence before Robin answers. Now her own tone is definitive.

"Both, honey. Both of you."

*   *   *

8

The sequence opens with a panoramic shot of Madeleine and four-year-old Austin in the close foreground, walking along the side of a paved coastal main road. Bright sapphire sea fills the screen behind them. Madeleine wears a formal dress with her hair up as before, covered with the Martinican head-tie, a leather handbag hanging from the bend of her arm. Her other arm reaches down to hold the hand of young Austin walking beside her, dressed in short pants and a neatly pressed white short-sleeve shirt, leather shoes and tall white socks.

The camera shifts to a shot from behind Madeleine and Austin, as they approach a single-story wooden office building at Docksite. There's an empty bench against the outside front wall. They climb the stoop and enter slowly, with a small bell attached to the inside of the door, containing a frosted glass pane with wire mesh molded in. The bell rings quietly as the door closes behind them.

We see an interior view of the sparse but affluent office, as viewed from the door: the impressive-looking counter of solid mahogany wood, polished to a shine, with a couple of desks in the space behind it, littered with papers. An old typewriter sits on one, chairs behind both desks. In the middle of the wall between the two desks is another door with the same panel of frosted, wiremesh-embedded glass, open, leading to an inner office. There are beams of striated and dusty late afternoon sunlight entering through the multiple side windows covered with glass jalousies.

From a side angle we watch Madeleine and young Austin approach the shining counter cautiously, standing there before it.

Barto enters from the inner office, wearing a white shirt with his sleeves rolled to mid-forearms, his tie loose at the collar. He smiles, steps around the counter and approaches Austin, bending to pat his head affectionately.

"Let's have a look at young Austin!"

Barto picks the boy up and puts him to sit on the counter, facing out. Madeleine stands to one side, Barto to the other.

She speaks with unrestrained pride.

"He just make he fourth birthday."

"A big man for four years ... he got your eyes."

"And your forehead. Your straight nose."

Barto turns toward Madeleine, looking into her face.

"Plenty obeah in those eyes - I could tell you!"

Her eyes brighten for an unmistakable instant, a flash; then we watch the light in them dim as her tone turns serious.

"You say in the message I must come. You say I must bring the child."

His tone is serious, too.

"Yes, I did want to ... see Austin before I go. And I did want to see you, Madeleine. One more time before - "

She interrupts, hastily.

"Where you going?"

Barto hesitates, his voice beginning to stumble.

"Quite to New York - Presbyterian Hospital."

Now her tone registers concern.

"You sick?"

This time Barto's hesitation is extended. He takes a deep breath, exhales slowly.

"I got a brain tumor. Doctors here can't do nothing. But in New York ... they could perform a operation."

"When you coming back?"

Barto smiles. As best he can.

"I'm not sure. I'll be gone . . . at least two-three months."

He hesitates again.

"If I lucky. Thing is, I have decided that if - WHEN I reach back, I go look proper into adopting Austin."

Another pause. She responds slowly, cautiously, sounding out each word.

"What you say?"

"Just so: he go take my name."

Madeleine is shocked into silence. She turns her head to the side, panicked, frightened - both for Barto and for her child. It's as though she's studying the strips of dusty sunlight filtering in through the jalousies. But in fact she doesn't see them at all. After a moment Barto reaches to her chin and gently turns her face back toward him, as they look into each other's eyes. Barto trying to smile, Madeleine remaining in shock. Eventually, he reaches into his pant's pocket and removes a clump of tightly-folded bills, colored a dirty jade, and holds them up to Madeleine - but she offers him no response. After several seconds Barto reaches toward the handbag hanging from her arm, opens it, and tucks the thick clump inside. He clasps the handbag shut with a loud click. Barto turns and lifts young Austin down from the counter.

"I go send for you when I reach back. I go send for Austin."

Madeleine takes Austin's hand and leads him to the door, a brief reflection of her stunned face in the meshed frosted-glass panel as she she turns the knob and pulls the door open, the bell ringing quietly.

Little Austin walks out. Madeleine follows, pulling the door closed behind her, the bell ringing quietly again.

*   *   *

9

Austin and Robin in their dining room, sitting on stools at the table from Maximos' treehouse (bare - no food, wine, or prescription vial).

Austin scratches his temple.

"That's crazy."

Robin looks at him with a slightly preoccupied grimace.

"Please don't say that, honey."

He continues, unperturbed.

"I mean, what's crazy is . . . I remember that scene exactly - Barto's face, his white shirt with the sleeves rolled up. I remember him lifting me and putting me to sit on the counter."

He takes a breath, resumes.

"I remember the salt-moss SMELL of Docksite through the jalousies."

Robin again treads the fine line of conscientious encouragement.

"Sounds like your - what did you call it? - your brain-seahorse is swimming along nice n' steady."

"Hippocampus."

"That's it."

Austin wanders back on track.

". . . thing that threw me was the adoption business."

Robin's face slips toward preoccupation again.

"Oh." She pauses, takes a stab. "But you never said anything bout Barto wanting to ADOPT you before."

"Because . . . in my memory there wasn't any sound . . . no conversation. Just the images - a silent movie."

He pauses, then continues.

"I never heard what Barto SAID to mummy . . . not till just now."

Robin is a little startled. She speaks slowly.

"And how do you feel about this . . . sudden revelation?"

"I don't know."

He hesitates.

"Guess I'm still shocked. Like Mummy was."

Her tone remains cautious.

"Yeah."

In contrast, Austin is steady and definitive.

"So that's it," he says.

Suddenly Robin is upset again, frustrated.

"WHAT'S it? I'm not in your head, Austin!"

"Mummy never saw Barto again. He never survived the operation. Barto
returned to Trinidad . . . only to be buried. Mummy took me to see his mausoleum
in Lapeyrouse Cemetery. And I went back once on my own, before I left the island
myself, at the age of eighteen . . . with my dream of becoming an actor."

He pauses, still pensive.

"But that's it . . . so far as Barto and mummy were concerned."

Robin finally surrenders. She smiles, caution to the wind.

"No it isn't," she says. "I really don't think it is."

Austin contorts his face.

"What do YOU mean?" he asks.

She smiles.

"Watch.

V

THE HAPPY ENDING

1

This scene takes up where the penultimate one left off: with Madeleine and young Austin standing outside Barto's office at Docksite. There's a wooden bench against the front wall of the building, and Madeleine lifts Austin and puts him to sit on it.

"You wait," she says. "I coming right back."

She turns from her son, climbs the stoop, and reenters the office, bell on the door ringing. We watch Madeleine approach the counter, waiting, and a moment later Barto enters from his inner office, still standing on the other side of the counter.

His voice sounds concerned.

"You forget something?"

Madeleine stands there with the counter between them, clutching her handbag, silently staring at him.

"You know," he says after several seconds. "I leaving tomorrow. I got plenty things to attend to."

She speaks evenly now, her voice the sound of conviction.

"Well you ain't too busy to hear what I got to say."

Barto is taken aback. He looks at her.

Madeleine continues.

"I come to tell you THIS child don't belong to you a-tall."

Another uncomfortable silence. Eventually, it's Barto who speaks – quickly, quietly.

"Then who the father is?"

Silence again. After several long seconds Madeleine responds, forcefully.

"Don't you say that. Don't you even SAY that. What you take me for? Some jamet?"

Barto looks at her, confused.

"Then WHO the child belong to?" he asks.

"Who you think?"

"I ain't ... "

"Me," Madeleine says. "Austin belong to me. Me ONE. Me ALONE. You could see he any time you want. When you reach back. You only got to send word. But don't you ever think for one second ... "

Another silence. Madeleine finally breaks down.

Barto's voice is gentle.

"Think what, Madeleine?"

"That you could take he way from me."

"I ain't ..."

"Only name Austin need – only name he ever go have – is mine."

Madeleine stands looking at him for another moment, then she turns toward the door. But after a step she hesitates, and turns around again, facing Barto – staring at him.

"You right," she says. "I DID forget something."

"Yes?"

"I forget this ... "

Madeleine opens her handbag, reaches in to grasp hold of the thick clump of bills, and with a broad sweep of her arm she hurls them high into the air. All the bills floating down around herself and Barto – all the air littered with them – twirling like leaves, a dirty glittering.

"If you ever feel you need a jamet in truth ... you could give that to SHE."

Madeleine closes her handbag with a loud click. She turns and exits, shutting the door behind her. With Barto still standing behind the shining, solid mahogany counter, bills scattered around him, dusty beams of striated sunlight filtering through the jalousies.

    The scene closes with a tight shot of the small bell attached to the inside of the door, ringing quietly.

*   *   *

2

The sequence opens with a close-up of Scavenger Bob's school bell, his arm reaching out through the driver window, ringing it vigorously. The camera pulls back to a panoramic shot of the desert outside Simian City, the school bus approaching, speeding along, filled with partying mutants - late afternoon sunshine. The bus slides in the desert sand, its red lights blinking, some of the mutants reaching out of the windows, now grasping wine bottles. Music blasts through the loudspeaker - Queen's "We Will Rock You."

Switch to a panoramic shot of Simian City, all of the apes still at work.
We hear the far off rumble of the bus, the shouting, music. As the bus slowly enters the frame in the distant, upper right background. It begins to circle the city - the apes pausing from their work, pointing, uncomprehending. We also see that the bus is again pulling the flatbed trailer, with the gray tarpaulin covering its full load.

Cut to a shot of the bus speeding along Main Street, its lights blinking, music blasting, the young apes and black children running behind it. With Maximos' treehouse in the left foreground.
The bus comes to a screeching halt beside Maximos' terrace. Scavenger Bob continues ringing his hand bell, the partying mutants leaning out of the windows, grasping their wine bottles, music blasting.
Through the windshield we watch Scavenger Bob halt his ringing, and over the music he blows the horn twice. He swings the stop sign out and the doors open with a rusty squeal. And Koch exits, striding confidently down the steps - he now wears the Obamite medallion around his neck, his shiny bald head exposed (no cap).
By this point Maximos has awoken from his nap, appearing at the edge of his terrace above, wearing his nightrobe. Also by this point all of the apes have gathered behind the bus, curious, beginning to surround it - some of the younger chimps and black youths already beginning to dance.
Now Homer stumbles out of the bus, careful not to spill his stemmed glass of wine - wearing Koch's red cap, but turned backward on his head (no medallion). Homer puts his arm affectionately around Koch, and the two make their way together to the back of the bus, standing bedside the flatbed trailer.
The camera draws in, still showing Maximos standing at the edge of his terrace above - Stoker, Eva and Mira now standing behind him.
After a second Koch whistles though his fingers.

KOCH
SHUEEE-WEEET!

He turns toward the bus and Bob, draws a finger across his throat – as Bob kills the music.

                    MAXIMOS
               Thank you. That
          vulgar composition was grating
              against my sensibilities
               ... physically.

He pauses, his ape face showing the familiar pained exasperation.

                    MAXIMOS
          Now maybe I'll be able to fall back asleep,
          and dream up a HAPPIER ending for this
               infernal flood of fanfiction!

                    KOCH
                  (smiles)
              Sorry to inform you,
          Maximos. But this ain't THE END
           – less you're referrin' to that
               highly contested theory
                of evolution.

                    MAXIMOS
               A matter of
            catechism, I'm sure.

                    KOCH
             Fact is Maximos, this
           here's what the bone-diggers
          – and their brain-digger amigos –
           call a "Primal History Scene."
           It marks the beginnin' of all
               CULTURE – for simians
                and mutants alike.

A brief pause while Homer downs the last swallow of wine remaining in his glass, then clears his throat.

                    HOMER
           My colleague and companion
          is quite correct, Maximos. Kindly
            allow me to illustrate –

He turns to the trailer and pulls off the tarpaulin dramatically, unveiling a tall stash of dusty wine crates.

                    HOMER
        What we have here - courtesy of Governor
        Kirk Sr's Imperial Cellar - is precisely 217
        crates of Henri Jayer Salvatori Grand Cru,
        Pinot Noir variety, from the Côte de Nuits
            region of Burgundy, France - 1973 -
            retails at approximately three-
                 thousand bucks a pop.

He reaches into one of the cases and takes up a bottle, blowing off the dust.

                    HOMER
        But do you know what feature of
        this vintage most impresses me, Maximos?

                   MAXIMOS
                 I wouldn't
              venture to guess.

                    HOMER
                It's screw-off.

He opens the bottle, pours some into his glass, sniffs the aroma, and holds it up.

                    HOMER
                This Maximos,
               is civilization!

          (he turns to the apes gathered
              behind and around him)

          Ladies and gentlemen,
             boys and girls
          - please help yourselves!

        (then he turns toward the bus)

        Maestro Bob ... MUSIC please!

Bob cranks up the music through the loudspeaker - now it's Prince "1999" -

while the mutants begin filing out of the bus and, together with the apes, they all descend on the stash of wine. In the midst of their drinking and dancing, several of the apes and mutants discretely exchange their medallions and caps (now worn backward).

On the terrace above Maximos, Eva, Stoker and Mira dance as well –

I was droolin'
When I wrote this
So sue me if
I go 2 fast*

* the late artist Prince here anticipates the suit which will be launched by his own lawyers against his mother over the original "dancing baby-Prince" YouTube video (Wikipedia, 21 April 2016)

3

The sequence opens with an exterior long shot of Austin in Studio City, mid-
afternoon, riding his bicycle from a distance toward the camera, along the street in
front of his home. The music on the sound track fades as we watch Austin peddling –

> Mommy, why does
> everybody have
> a bomb?
> (repeat twice)

The camera steps back, still centered on Austin riding, revealing the
school bus in the lower left foreground. It comes to a halt with its red lights
blinking, as the stop sign extends (no bell); and Maximos and Eva (as chimpanzees)
are seen standing before their home. The bus doors swing open and young Mira
exits, climbing down the steps and running toward her parents, wearing her Hulk
backpack and carrying her Hulk lunchpail.

Close-up of Austin, riding past the blinking bus, turning and pulling
into his driveway – as we catch a parting glimpse of Scavenger Bob, wearing his
goggles, seated in driver's seat.

The camera shifts to a shot of Austin, leaning his bike against the wall at
the side of his home. It follows in a tracking shot as he walks around the house,
past the black Toyota with its peeling "Obama – we'll never forget" bumper sticker,
his hands free, no script under his arm.

Austin pauses as he reaches for his doorknob, looking back over his
shoulder. And the camera switches to his point-of-view: Maximos (now as human)
with his ten-year-old son perched on his shoulders, the boy wearing his Hulk
backpack, white tee-shirt and shorts with sneakers and tall white socks, his
navy L.A. Dodgers baseball cap turned backward on his head; and Eva (also human),

holding her son's Hulk lunchpail, her other arm around her husband's waist. The family walk together toward the door of their home.

All smile, as the boy waves to Austin.

Cut to a close-up of Austin – he turns his head and enters his home, closing the door behind him.

Fade to an interior shot of Robin, smartly dressed from work. She's seated at the wrought-iron dining table from the film's opening sequence, surrounded by its three other iron chairs. Robin is busy counting out Austin's pills into a plastic weekly medicine dispenser, as he enters the frame and takes a seat across from her. There's the small wicker basket with bananas on the table, the bottle of red wine, and two half-filled stemmed glasses.

Austin has the first line, while he pulls the chair under him.

"You're early."

She looks up from her pill-counting.

"Nona won the suit."

He considers this a moment.

"Small step for man . . . giant leap for the artist."

"Maybe," she says. "If Marvin were still around to claim some of it."

Austin reflects again.

"Guess his music is his memory."

Robin slides the dispenser over.

"Here . . . so you don't lose yours."

She also places two blue pills on the table before him.

"Starting today."

Austin frowns.

"Tomorrow morning I'll drink some more of mummy's memory tea." As he speaks he looks around the kitchen for his ziplock, "Only I can't remember where I left it."

Robin is forthright.

"Drink all the tea you want. But you're takin' these pills, too."

There's a short silence before Austin's face resumes its usual pensive expression.

"So here's the question ... "

Robin rolls her eyes, preparing herself for another of Austin's ruminations.

He continues undeterred.

"Do those pills - and mummy's tea, for that matter - keep me from losing my memory? Or do they prevent me from finding it?"

Robin shakes her head, frustration creeping in.

"Say again?"

"What we've just witnessed ... Barto and Mummy. All the rest. Those pills might've kept me from conjuring it up."

He pauses.

"IF I'd remembered to take them."

Robin breathes deep, releases.

"I suppose. But the real question is: what do you think about all of it, honey?"

Another pause.

"I'm not altogether sure. Guess I'm still processing it, like Mommy was."

She rolls her eyes again, unsure of what he's referring to.

"Yeah," she says.

Austin continues.

"Barto remains something of an enigma. Though I learned a few significant things about him."

"I suppose that's good. What about your momma?"

"I'd always sensed Mummy did the best she could for me. Within the realm of possibility. Now I know for sure."

"And what about you, Austin? How does all that make you feel about YOU?"

"Guess I have ... a better sense of where I came from. Of my place in the world."

"Good."

"... my 'legitimacy' thing," he adds.

Robin looks at him.

"But what does that really mean, Austin? To you? What's it mean to be 'legitimate'?"

Austin answers without a beat of hesitation.

"To have agency. To be granted agency."

Robin considers this.

"But Austin, you've had that all your life. It's the way you move in the world. It's what attracted me to you in the first place. What I fell in love with forty-three years ago!"

Austin smiles, almost a chuckle.

"My actor self, sure."

There's a momentary silence.

"I'd be willing to counter that," she says. "But go ahead."

His expression turns serious.

"Don't you see, Robin. I had to become an actor - a middle-class black, coming from a colonial background like I did - I had no choice."

He pauses.

"Had no choice NOT to be good at it, either. Something I learned from an early age."

There's a look of pleasure on Robin's face; it lights up for an instant.

"Your other self, other skin. The innocent, confused one that belonged to that young boy. That's the one who needed validation."

Austin smiles too.

"Exactly," he says.

But something else occurs to him.

"Or NOT exactly ... I needed the agency for my white self, my white skin. Cause when you're split down the middle, like I am, it's no longer given as a matter of principle ... handed to you on a silver platter."

Austin takes a breath, continues.

"The other side, other part – that middle-class, black, colonial-masquerader part – I was always pretty good at ... even as a boy."

"Like you're good at dichotomizing, Austin." She pauses. "You got to allow yourself a few uneasy contradictions. And 83's about time. Seems to me THAT'S what this is all about."

She corrects herself.

"One thing it's about, anyway."

Austin frowns, like somehow he's been hoodwinked.

Robin is fervent.

"So take your pills."

He protests.

"Wait a minute ... "

"Now that you got your memory, you don't want to lose it again ... "

Robin interrupts herself, smiles.

" – And I don't wanna come home and find you swingin' from the oak tree out front!"

He exhales a breath, takes up the pills.

"You win . . . but I'm sure going to miss those boys."

Her face suddenly drops. She draws out the word.

"Who?" she asks.

"Maximos and Homer. Cause if Simian City's nothing but a figment of my paranoid fantasy – or dementia – then they are too."

She looks at him, relieved.

"Austin, those goons'll be waiting for you at StarBucks. Right where you left 'em. Along with all the other out-of-work actors in Hollywood."

She raises her glass.

Austin smiles.

"Guess you're right about that, too."

He puts the pills in his mouth, touches his glass against hers.

As they drink, knocking is heard at the front door, offstage. Austin puts his glass down.

"I'll get it." He pushes back his chair.

Cut to a shot of Austin, looking out through the peephole of his front door, rounded at the top.

The camera switches to his point-of-view: we see the distorted image of a monster bearing an enormous barrel-chest, tiny dark pin-head above, two tiny pin-feet below. Behind the bars of the wrought-iron grille, it looks like a big hairy fish snagged in a net.

Switch to a shot over Austin's shoulder as he opens the door, and we see a broadly smiling Homer (as orangutan), fully restored. He's himself now, offset – not wearing his bling medallion or red baseball cap. Homer holds Austin's ziplock in one hand, in the other a primitive-looking instrument – musical? – made from a molded Coke bottle, elaborate seedpod and thin bamboo reed, with two eagle feathers dangling from it.

Switch to the reverse shot over Homer's shoulder – Austin stands in his doorway with the small, circular foyer behind him.

Homer raises up the ziplock.

"I believe this package of ganja belongs to you, Stoker."

Austin looks at him, puzzled.

Homer explains.

"You left it in your bicycle basket."

Austin takes the ziplock.

"Thanks, but it's not – "

Switch to the reverse shot over Austin's shoulder: Homer holds his instrument – with the front yard showing in the background, overgrown grass and the mossy oak with its undersized tire hanging by the length of old rope. He cuts Austin off.

" – And please take advantage of my ancient Hopi medicine pipe."

Austin shakes his head, confused.

"Your what?" he asks.

Homer smiles.

"My Barack Obonga – as verified by his birth certificate."

Austin is further confounded.

"For what purpose, Homer?"

"It's used to communicate with the ancestral spirits. A perfectly legal pastime in this state."

Homer holds out his instrument toward Austin and the camera with a hairy hand, gold Harvard school ring shining on his finger. He smiles.

"Memory is never to be trusted!"

FADE OUT

<u>END</u>

ROLL CREDITS: after the lion's roar, as the credits continue to roll, Queen (with Bowie) "Under Pressure" slowly comes up on the sound track –

This is our last dance
This is ourselves
Under pressure*

* Film Credits: www.robertantoni.com/credits

CODA

After the credits roll through, and the music fades completely – just as
we reach for our faux-velvet armrests with the intention of rising – the camera
brightens unexpectedly from a primordial and finely-flickering murk: it reveals
a darkened, 70's-ish, popcorn-plastered bedroom ceiling. Dimmed sunlight spreading
across from the right side of the frame, as though filtered through a gauzy
curtain.

Evocative, for the moment, of undulating dunes.

Beneath the vibrating wire of ciçadas-shrill, we make out the chirping of
early morning birds.

After a few seconds we hear Austin's now-familiar voice – tentative,
groggy, searching.

"Robin?"

Several more seconds of the birds chirping. We hear his voice again, a little
louder.

"Robin . . . you awake?"

Few more seconds of the birds.

"Yeah. I am now."

Robert Antoni is equal parts Trinidadian, Bahamian and US citizen. His first novel, Divina Trace (Quartet, 1991), received the Commonwealth Writers Prize, a National Endowment for the Arts Grant, and is recognized as a landmark in Caribbean writing. His other books are Blessed is the Fruit (Faber), My Grandmother's Erotic Folktales (Faber), Carnival (Faber), which was shortlisted for the Commonwealth Writers Prize 2006, and As Flies to Whatless Boys (Peepal Tree Press), which garnered the OCM Bocas Prize for Best Book 2014. Antoni is the recipient of a Guggenheim Fellowship and the NALIS Lifetime Achievement Award from the Trinidad and Tobago National Library.

author photograph Ali Bujnowski